THEO AND THE FESTIVAL OF SHADOWS

MICHAEL LA RONN

Published by Author Level Up LLC.

Version 2.0

Cover Design: J. Caleb Clark.

Editing: Maya Myers and Call Allen.

To get notifications when Michael releases new work, join his Fan Club atÂ www.michaellaronn.com/fanclub.

The ebook edition of this book is interactive. This print edition contains the author's favorite choices from the ebook edition. You can learn more about the ebook edition by visiting www.michaellaronn.com/theoandthefestivalofshadows

To Teddy.

Thanks for keeping me safe from the monsters under the bed all these years.

THEO AND THE FESTIVAL OF SHADOWS

1

SINISTER SUNDOWN

Theo woke up in a puddle of dirty water.

He propped himself up against a box and rubbed his head. He was in the basement, and it was dark. He had been in the basement many times, but this time the darkness changed it. The stacks of boxes and old furniture, which looked normal during the day, now took strange shapes. Scary shadows danced against the wall—claws, fangs, and wings that seemed as if they wanted to rip him apart.

The cement floor was cold, and he hugged himself to keep warm. The stale, damp air made him cough. He struggled to take a deep breath. He tried to focus his eyes, but everything hovered around him as if he were in a waking dream. Through the window above, he could see the pink and orange rays of sunset burning through blades of grass.

A shadow swept over the basement, and he realized it was dusk.

Grant is unprotected. I've got to get upstairs before nightfall.

He staggered toward the stairs, the grogginess lifting as he padded across the room. He passed the old crib, tall and nefarious in the low light; he had lain there with Grant during afternoon naps, snuggling up against him as the mobile lulled them both to sleep. That was a long time ago. The crib had once belonged to Grant's older brother, Shawn, and he remembered how Shawn had never snuggled with him. Shawn's teenage face, brown and pimpled, flashed through Theo's mind, sneering at him; it was the same sneer he had worn before he'd launched Theo into the basement.

But he didn't want to think about that right now. He climbed the wooden steps, one by one, hoisting himself onto each stair with all his strength. He jumped and grabbed the golden doorknob, but it wouldn't turn.

Please open.

He knocked, but his furry paws didn't make a sound. He threw himself against the door—nothing but a soft thud.

An old sneaker lay near the door. He pounded the door with it, and soon he heard footsteps on the other side. He dropped to the floor and went stiff.

Mom opened the door. She wore a green sweater and blue jeans, and her curly red and black micro braids hung down to her shoulders. She studied Theo, peering at him from underneath her glasses.

"Theo, what are you doing down here?"

She picked him up, inspected him, and clucked her tongue. "Shawn, did you throw Theo in the basement?"

Shawn was sitting at the kitchen table doing his ninth-grade algebra homework. He wore a hoodie and baggy jeans.

"Yeah. Grant needs to grow up," he said.

Mom carried Theo to the kitchen sink, rinsed the dirt from his ears, and dried him with a paper towel. She set him on the counter and smiled. As she turned back to Shawn, still angry, Theo looked out into the backyard, where the sun was sinking into the horizon.

"I can't believe you," Mom said to Shawn. "Theo was yours when you were little, remember?"

Shawn puffed. "I don't need a teddy bear anymore. Unlike my pathetic brother."

Mom gave Shawn a death stare.

"We made a bet," Shawn said. "I dared him to spend one night without Theo to prove that he was a man."

"A man! He's nine years old!"

"He hasn't cried like a baby yet, so maybe he's finally growin' up."

Mom continued her lecture as Shawn went back to his homework and ignored her. When they weren't looking, Theo jumped off the counter and dashed into the hallway.

I'm almost there.

He ran to the stairs leading up to the second floor. He could hear Grant playing in his room upstairs, making noises and crashing sounds with the other toys.

Good. He's still there.

He had just climbed onto the bottom stair when he heard a sudden bark. Amos, the family bulldog, charged down the hall and took Theo in his jaws.

"No, no, no, you stupid brute," Theo said, punching Amos on the nose. "Can't you see that it's sunset? Don't you know what will happen if I don't make it upstairs?"

The dog panted and trotted into the living room, where Dad was sitting on the couch reading a book about African-American history. He wore a white button-up shirt and khakis with brown dress socks. He was deep in thought, stroking his beard with one hand while occasionally making notes on the pages.

Amos set Theo at Dad's feet and barked. Theo went stiff again, and Dad picked him up.

"What are you doing down here, Theo? Let's get you upstairs where you belong."

Dad had almost reached Grant's room when Mom called him.

"Honey, can you explain to Shawn that he can't keep teasing his brother?"

"He doesn't need to explain nothin'!" Shawn shouted.

Dad set Theo on a table and jogged back downstairs.

Theo jumped down from the table and ran to Grant's room, where Grant was playing. His short, nappy hair stood out in unruly tufts, and he wore a green-and-white-striped rugby. He was missing a few teeth.

A twin bed surrounded by toys sat in the middle of the room, and posters of Grant's favorite superheroes hung crooked on the sky-blue walls.

"Listen up," Grant said. He held Nora the Boombox in one hand. She was orange and oval-shaped, with a CD drive on her head and a microphone attached to her side.

In his other hand, Grant held an action figure with long blond hair and a leather jacket. He moved the hero close to the microphone and pretended to speak for him.

"Come out with your hands up."

There was a pause, and nothing happened. Grant frowned, and then tugged a string that stretched behind the bed. A spinning top rolled out, blinking and dancing in a circle.

"Okay," Grant said, now speaking for the top, "You got me."

"We trusted you," James the Action Hero said. "And you betrayed us."

"I needed the money," the Top said. "And now you will see what I did with it!"

Grant ran to the other side of the room. He pulled a tow truck out of the toy box and threw it in front of the spinning top.

"You again?" Tompkins the Tow Truck said as Grant guided him toward James. "You gave me a beating back in '73. I haven't forgotten that. I hope you like pepperoni on your Tombstone, because I'm going to grind you into road pizza."

James the Action Figure pounded his fists together and posed; Grant pushed a button on his back and the brass knuckles painted on James's hands glowed.

Grant sighed and shook James to make him speak. "If we had Theo with us, this battle would have already been over."

James and Tompkins the Tow Truck circled each other, and Theo relaxed as he watched Grant play.

He's safe.

Grant raised Tompkins into the air and yelled "Vroom!"

Outside, the horizon swallowed the sun, and a shadow fell over the room. Purple clouds billowed from beneath the bed, choking Grant. A booming laugh echoed as the room filled with smoke.

"It can't be—" Theo cried.

Grant screamed.

Theo charged into the smoke just in time to see two wispy hands around Grant's waist. They pulled the boy under the bed, leaving behind a portal of purple smoke.

Stratus.

Theo jumped onto a large ball and threw himself onto the bed. He reached behind the pillow, grabbed his wooden sword and shield, and dropped down to the floor. He was about to enter the portal when he heard a voice.

"Theo, don't go."

Topperson, the spinning top, spun in place as he spoke. The rest of the toys cowered behind him.

"You'll never make it out alive. Grant is Stratus's property now."

"You failed to protect him," Theo said, not turning around. "You have no right to speak."

"How could we resist? He would have killed us all."

Topperson spun across the floor and stopped in front of Theo. His insides lit up as if they were on fire. "Theo, that portal goes to the Stratusphere. It's no place for a toy."

"It's no place for Grant, either."

"It's an evil place. Shadows lurk in every corner. I am lucky to have escaped." Topperson spun closer, showing a deep cut across his face, but Theo pushed him aside.

"Stratus is going to pay."

A roar came from the portal, and an ogre with a club climbed out. He had three cloudy eyes, scaly orange skin, and wore ripped overalls. He dwarfed Theo.

The other toys screamed and climbed into the toy box as the ogre roared again.

"Stratus has sent a toy from the other side to destroy us," Topperson said.

Theo jumped back and readied his sword. "He won't stop me," he said, slanting his eyes. He slashed at the ogre, but the wooden sword bounced off the ogre's leg and Theo stumbled backward.

The ogre laughed and raised his club.

"Uh oh," Theo breathed.

Theo rolled out of the way just in time, and the club smashed the floor, shaking the room. The quake took the ogre by surprise, and he wobbled on one foot.

Theo ran to the toy box to regroup as the ogre stomped toward him. A slingshot jumped down and insinuated itself against his thigh.

"David and Goliath, eh?" Theo said. He grabbed the slingshot, slung an agate marble, and aimed. The marble hit one of the ogre's eyes, and the beast dropped the club.

Tompkins the Tow Truck sped out of the closet and grabbed the club with his tow hooks. Theo jumped on the back of the truck and they reversed, driving the club into the ogre's stomach and causing him to stumble backward, winded. Just as he was about to fall into the portal, the ogre sprang forward and belly flopped onto the floor. He reached up, ripped the club from Tompkins, and threw him and Theo against the wall.

"Ouch . . ." Tompkins said. Then he passed out.

Theo staggered up and looked around, then spotted a toy airplane hiding under a sock in the middle of the room. He was painted like a green fighter jet, with a three-wing propeller on his nose. When they made eye contact, Planeby whispered "Sssh."

Theo decided to commandeer the plane. He lifted the sock, and Planeby shushed him louder. "You're going to get me killed."

"You should be offering your services for Grant's sake," Theo said. He jumped inside the airplane and turned on the engine.

"Please, no—"

"Be quiet!"

Planeby screamed as Theo eased into the air. "I'm gonna die! I'm gonna die!"

"You will if you keep talking like that," Theo said, fanning to the left.

The ogre saw them and roared.

Come on. Throw your club at me. Do it!

The ogre raised the club as if to throw it. Theo rolled the plane to the right, and Planeby started crying.

Come on.

The ogre grabbed a nearby ball and threw it at the plane. Theo fired a rubber missile and sent the ball to the floor.

"Phew," Theo said. He circled the room, and the ogre turned to keep facing them. Theo waited until the ogre's back was to the portal, then he steered the plane down.

"Noooo," Planeby said. "We're gonna hit him!"

SMASH! The impact knocked the ogre into the portal. The force broke off Planeby's propeller, and he and Theo fell to the ground and rolled across the floor.

"I'm broken," Planeby said. "It's your fault, Theo!"

Theo pulled himself up. "You should be honored. Grant will appreciate your sacrifice."

"Have you no compassion?" Planeby asked. "I'm a collector's item! They'll never be able to find a replacement propeller." Several toys gathered and tried to console him, patting his wings as he sniffled.

"Hmph," Theo said, facing the portal.

Topperson spun from the shadows. "Well done, Theo. But that ogre is just a hint of what you will encounter in the Stratusphere."

"I'm ready," Theo said. "Stratus will never forget this day—the day he is defeated by me, an Ursabrand!"

He jumped into the portal.

2

SMOKE BETWEEN THE EYES

Shadows formed into a vortex around Theo, and he zoomed headfirst through them until he crashed onto an invisible floor. The impact sent a purple shockwave in all directions, causing scary shapes and odd-looking buildings to spring up before the darkness swallowed them again.

He yelled for Grant, but his voice lost its way.

Believing that he saw Grant's silhouette ahead, Theo pulled himself up into a half-run, half-crawl.

"Grant . . ."

But the shadows suffocated him. He fell on his back, shaking as several versions of Grant's face circled him. They were happy, mad, sad, crying.

"Save me!"

"I hate you!"

"I'm scared . . ."

"You're a useless teddy bear."

He reached for the faces, but they dissolved at his touch until there was one left—a scowling, angry face.

"I don't need you anymore," Grant said.

"Yes, you do—"

"No. I'm a man."

"But I'm your best buddy," Theo said.

"No! You never were."

"Stratus has poisoned you."

"No," Grant said, frowning. "You've poisoned me. I hope you die."

The face exploded and Theo screamed. It had to be an illusion; he couldn't accept that Grant was gone.

The shadows grew thicker, and it was getting harder to breathe.

"Stratus," he said, gasping, "Show yourself, so that I may vanquish you from existence."

Silence.

"I'm an Ursabrand!" Theo cried, and his words faded on their way to nowhere. "You can't defeat me!"

Stratus rumbled out of the darkness. He appeared small at first, but soon he towered several stories above Theo. His head was wispy, made of shifting shadows, and his two red eyes glared. He sneered at Theo and let out a booming laugh. His torso was a wall of shadow and fog; where there should have been feet, only darkness swirled. In one hand he clutched Grant by the waist. The boy was asleep. Stratus grabbed Theo by the neck with the other hand, and squeezed hard.

Theo tried to pry himself free, but he couldn't. The grip crushed him; he had never felt anything so strong. Stratus's laughter grew louder, and Theo's vision grew dimmer.

I'm sorry, Grant. I failed you.

Theo took a final breath and gave in to Stratus. He drifted away into deeper darkness where nothing mattered. He felt light and free. He closed his eyes, thinking of Grant and their playtimes together.

He heard a voice, but it was muffled and sounded like it was underwater. Then a flash cut through the darkness, followed seconds later by an explosion.

Stratus let go. Feeling gushed back into Theo's body, and all of his memories surged across his vision like the screen of a mad kaleidoscope.

"Wake up!" cried the strange voice. It grew louder and deeper. Feminine. Theo ignored it and tried to remember Grant's face.

The darkness that had become so familiar to him condensed itself into one black eye, and he saw a purple face staring down at him—a round, furry face with a mouth that kept screaming: "Wake up, wake up, wake up—"

Theo shot up and sucked in air, and the purple bear smacked him on the back.

"Keep breathing," she said. "Don't think. Just breathe. You've got to get the nightmares out. There!" Her voice was deep and throaty, and she looked just like him. Almost.

When Theo exhaled again, he saw that he was in a field of dead grass, withered and brown. The calm night sky above was starry and navy blue, and the moon, an enormous yellow crescent, glowed from behind a cloud. The air was desolate and had a tinge of sadness that he couldn't comprehend. It scared him.

The purple bear hovered above him—literally. She had one eye and a peeling X of white tape where the other eye had been. Her entire left arm was wrapped in bandages that looked ratty, as if they had been there for a long time.

"That was close. Stratus almost had you."

Theo keeled over, unable to speak.

"What are you doing traveling through the Stratusphere alone?" she asked, floating around him as she spoke. "Are you from the other side? You must be. You look so clean and fresh, how I used to look. I was so beautiful once, too. So plushy." She laughed to herself and sighed. "And look at me now."

"Shut up," Theo said finally, exhaling. "You ruined it. I could have defeated him."

"He almost killed you!"

Theo leaped up and shook her. "Tell me where Stratus is!"

She tried to hover away, but Theo held tight. "Quit flying around and tell me where Stratus is, or I'll—"

"You'll what?"

Theo drew his wooden sword. It was broken from his encounter with Stratus, but he raised it anyway and threatened to stab. "This is your last chance—"

The purple bear yelled, and blue energy formed on the tips of her paws. She zapped Theo with a ball of blue light that sent him halfway across the field. His sword fell into the grass, and his wooden shield flew up out of his hands and conked him on the head.

"Ow . . ."

"That's what you get. If you try that again, I'll fire another dream blast at you. I saved your life, you know."

"Thanks for nothing," Theo said, rubbing his head. "Make yourself truly useful and tell me where I can find Grant."

The purple bear dropped her hands and the energy on her fingertips faded. "So stubborn and headstrong. We're definitely related."

"We couldn't possibly be related."

"You're an Ursabrand, like me. I'm Lucinda," she said, offering Theo her paw.

He stared at her bandaged arm and scoffed. "Some Ursabrand you are."

"If you only knew. I've been here for so long, I've forgotten what it's like on the other side." She suddenly looked very nervous. "Oh no. You're here because Stratus has your owner."

Theo nodded.

"It happened to me, too," Lucinda said. "My owner was

playing, and then the next thing I knew, Stratus snatched her, and I followed her here."

"Where is your owner?"

Lucinda hung her head. "It doesn't matter now. But you should have come sooner."

"I was preoccupied with an ogre."

She pointed to a clock tower that rose from a huge castle on the horizon. The castle was very far away, yet it seemed to dominate the sky. It had several spires and was made of dull gray stones. "Twelve hours until sunrise."

"And?"

"If you don't rescue your owner by then, you'll end up like me—trapped."

Theo felt queasy. He was stuck in this strange place with this strange bear, and now she had told him that he had a limited amount of time to rescue Grant. It was too much. Fear sank into his legs and shook them, but he tried not to show it.

The sound of wheels in the distance distracted Theo from his thoughts. He turned to see a covered wagon approaching, pulled by toy horses with matted manes and lame legs. A strongman with big, shiny muscles, a black-and-white-striped shirt, and painted-on muttonchops drove the wagon; other strange-looking, maimed toys hung out from the sides, staring at Theo.

"Lucinda," the strongman said with a lilting German accent, "you all right?"

Lucinda smiled and waved to the caravan. "I rescued him."

The wagon came to a stop, and the toys surrounded Theo and Lucinda. The strongman, who kept flexing his muscles as if his inner gears were malfunctioning, stood grinning at Theo. He was joined by a cowgirl wearing jeans, a red button-up shirt, a yellow cowboy hat, and a winsome smile that seemed as if she didn't care about her appearance, despite the gash across her face. Next to her, a white, wobbly, robotic dachshund with one blue eye and one red eye panted. His tail clicked as he wagged it. Slowly, other broken toys with interesting faces and injuries joined them.

"A new visitor," Heinrich the strongman said. He bent forward and flexed his biceps for Theo. "How do you like my rippling muscles?"

The cowgirl twirled a lasso in the air and yelled, "Yippie ki-yay! I'm Bethany."

The robotic dog barked and said in a stilted electronic voice, "My name is Shaggy. I am pleased to make your acquaintance."

The toys did tricks in front of Theo and tried to get his attention; it was information overload.

Theo stepped backward and then fell down, hard. He wanted to get away.

Lucinda hovered around the group and clapped her hands together; a sonic boom silenced everyone.

"Stop! You're going to scare him more than he is already."

Theo stumbled to his feet. "I'm not scared."

"Of course you are," Lucinda said.

Heinrich raised his hand. "Yes, I've been here for an eternity, and I want to pee my pants every day."

"Nobody lives in the Stratusphere who ain't scared," Bethany said.

"Indeed. Nothing here is what it seems," Shaggy said. His red eye pulsed violently. "Stratus watches everyone. He is omnipresent. Those who bow down to him are bestowed favors. Those who resist him suffer a fate worse than death. Like us. We are forced to wander the countryside in constant fear."

"I am Theodorus Ursabrand," Theo said, puffing out his chest. "I am descended from a long line of courageous bears for whom nothing is too scary, for whom no monster is too strong. I have—"

"—taken an oath to defend my owner, even if it means sacrificing my life," Lucinda interrupted. "Yeah, yeah. I can recite the whole oath, too. If you're such a successful Ursabrand, then why are you here?"

"I was talking before you butted in." Theo looked at the other toys and said, "I will face Stratus, defeat him, and free all of you from this forsaken land."

Lucinda fell out of the air, laughing. "You can't save us. We're condemned."

"You are condemned because your mind is weak. But I wasn't talking to you. Any real Ursabrand would have destroyed Stratus by now."

The other toys whispered among themselves.

"He is very brave," Heinrich said.

"Yeah, maybe he can save us," Shaggy said.

"But what about the festival?" Bethany asked. "We've got to put on the festival."

"Tell me where to find Stratus," Theo said.

Heinrich pointed to the castle. "But you'll never get in. If you try to step through the front gate, you'll be turned into teddy bear sausage. You should stay for our festival. Yes, that's much better! Don't worry yourself about that castle. No, don't do that!"

"I don't care about your stupid festival."

"We might be willing to help you," Lucinda said. "That is, if you were willing to help us."

"Why would I help an Ursabrand imposter like you?"

"Because I can get you into the castle."

Theo stomped toward Lucinda. "Then tell me how."

"I saved your life. You owe me."

"Yes, you owe her," Heinrich said. "Uh-huh, yes you do!"

"Besides," Lucinda said, "My plan involves using some

things that we don't currently have. We could use some help, couldn't we, everyone?"

"Yes."

"Oh god, yes!"

"Yesiree!"

Heinrich bear-hugged Theo. "My brave little bear. You're going to help us make the festival a success!"

Theo sighed, but he knew this place was dangerous. It would be suicide to storm the castle now.

These toys are weird, but maybe they can help.

"What do you want me to do?" he asked.

"Get to know us and we'll tell you," Lucinda said. She pointed at the clock tower. "There are twelve hours until sunrise. It seems like a lot of time, but it's not, really. Still, I'm confident that we can finish everything by then, but it'll depend on you, Theo."

She hovered away. "Since you're so brave and strong, it shouldn't be a problem for you. Heinrich will tell you what to do."

Theo frowned at her.

I'd better get started.

Theo approached Heinrich, and the strongman clapped with glee.

"I've lost my Whatsamadoozle," Heinrich said. "I, the mighty Heinrich, am nothing without it."

"What's a Whatsamadoozle?"

Heinrich looked offended. "What isn't a Whatsamadoozle?"

"Why don't you go and find it?"

"I must protect the caravan," he said. "If those rival toys come, I will give them ouchies. But you're a supple little teddy bear. Maybe you can find it for me."

Theo rolled his eyes. "Where is it?"

Heinrich pointed to a dark forest in the distance. "We just

came through the Evil Woods. It must have fallen off the wagon while we were there."

"Fine. I'll help you find your whatsamathingy."

"It's a Whatsamadoozle, you silly bear. Oh, you're a miracle dressed in fur! It will be the easiest quest ever. Just look for the golden glow and you will find it. You'll be back in ten minutes."

Heinrich lifted Theo into the air, aimed him at the Evil Woods, and launched him with the force of a cannon. Theo shielded his hands in front of his face as he arced into the air and crashed through the trees.

3

QUEST FOR THE WHATSAMADOOZLE

The Evil Woods were covered in shadows, and Theo could hardly see. The trees were black; their wiry branches blocking most of the moonlight. Even though they looked dead, they seemed alive.

Theo heard strange rustlings everywhere, as if something were waiting in the darkness to reach out and grab him. There was no path, so he had to climb, duck, and swing his way through the undergrowth.

After a while, he saw a golden glow in the distance.

This quest was easier than I thought.

He ran toward the glow, but it seemed to bounce away the closer he got. Eventually, he caught up with it, and discovered that the glow was coming from a huge golden mallet being dragged across the ground by a purple pterodactyl with serrated teeth, sharp wings, and bony feet. The mallet made a thrashing sound as it passed over the dead grass, and every stomp from the pterodactyl shook the ground.

Theo ducked behind a nearby tree, his heart thumping.

"Yes," the dinosaur said in his raspy voice, admiring the mallet. "what a remarkable find. Stratus will be pleased."

He tossed the mallet into the air, where it flashed and became a golden trophy. Grabbing the trophy by the handles, the dinosaur blushed and acted like he was on stage receiving it. "No, Your Grace, I can't accept this marvelous trophy. I'm a simple toy. So simple! I just want your love and affection. I don't want money, I don't want gifts."

The trophy materialized into a statue of the dinosaur, with a grin even uglier than in real life. "All I want is a statue of myself in your courtyard to show all these pathetic toys in this dimension that I, Cutter, am your most faithful servant. Yes, I will serve you until the end of my days . . ."

He's crazy, completely crazy. And he's three times my size.

Cutter grew tired of his revelry and growled. The statue morphed into a huge scythe, and he threw it ahead of him, where it mowed down several trees and returned to him like a boomerang. He caught it and then slashed another tree in half, laughing as it fell.

"I should be more conservative. I'll eliminate half the forest at this rate. And then where will I hide and wait for unsuspecting toys so that I can slice them into atoms?"

Cutter pivoted and stomped in Theo's direction. Startled, Theo stepped backward and stepped on a twig.

Cutter stopped. "Who's there?"

Theo stumbled from behind the tree, his legs shaking. "G-give me the Whatsamadoozle."

"The what?"

"In your hand. Surrender it, and I will spare you." Theo drew his broken sword.

"You call that piece of timber a sword?" Cutter asked, laughing demonically. He morphed the Whatsamadoozle into a gigantic sword that he could hardly wield. "This is a sword." He raised it as if to strike, but then lowered it and morphed it into a golden mallet again. "Let's try this Whatsamathingamajiggybob —on you."

Cutter smacked Theo with the mallet, sending him flying into the air. As Theo fell into another section of the forest, Cutter's voice echoed through the trees: "If I see you again, it will be the end of you, bear."

* * *

Theo crawled out of a bush, shaking sticks and branches from his fur.

"This is getting old," he said, rubbing his head. He looked in the direction where he thought Cutter had been, but there was only darkness.

Suddenly, the trees around him lumbered awake and stood up on their roots. They groaned and began walking all around him, forcing him to jump out of the way before they stepped on him. After a minute, they stopped, sat on their roots, and laughed with their wooden, sinewy laughter.

Theo glanced around, but he was even less sure of his bearings now.

"I won't be fooled," he said, and hurried in what he hoped was the right direction.

As he ran, he heard a cry.

"Help me!"

In the distance, a toy raccoon darted frantically among the trees.

A tree grinned evilly, and prepared to step on the raccoon with its snake-like roots.

Theo knew he had to save the toy. He stumbled through the undergrowth toward it. "Take my hand," he said.

The raccoon's eyes glowed orange, and then it laughed.

"Praise Stratus!" it cried, disappearing into a wisp of smoke.

A tree smacked Theo with a branch, and he lost his bearing.

"Crap."

Dazed, Theo continued in the direction he thought was correct, but he felt as if he were going in circles.

"I lost my way."

He refused to give up. He kept running, hoping for any sort of sign or clue. Finally, after what seemed like forever, he saw a golden glow through the trees, and he ran toward it.

Theo poked through the last tree, and he entered a clearing with a large stone dais in the middle. Cutter was sitting atop the dais, playing with the Whatsamadoozle.

"Yes, Your Grace, I am your most faithful servant. I hope that you will give me a lisssssome little boy to feast upon. Perhaps that nappy-headed little boy you brought in this evening."

Grant.

Theo wanted to charge the dais.

If he touches Grant, I will hurt him really badly.

"What do you do with all the little boys and girls you bring to your castle, Your Grace? I want to know. If you aren't eating them, then perhaps you can give me a few morsels . . ."

Cutter dragged the Whatsamadoozle to the other side of the dais, and he turned his back.

Theo crept toward the dais and tripped over something. Looking down, he saw that he had stepped on a wooden leg. Scattered about the clearing in large mounds were toy parts—heads, eyes, legs, and feet of toys whose lives Cutter had ended. Theo felt his stomach in his mouth.

He searched the field for something he could use, and settled on another wooden sword.

He peeked over the top of the dais; Cutter was still monologuing to himself. He climbed up and aimed the sword at Cutter's head.

"Hey!" Theo cried.

Cutter turned around, and the sword hit his eye. "Arrrrgh—" He clutched his face with one hand. With the other hand, he transformed the Whatsamadoozle into a battle ax, and he swung it blindly.

Theo dove over the ax, and Cutter missed him. He ran under Cutter's legs, but the dinosaur spun around, smacking him with the ax.

"Pesky little bear," Cutter said. He approached Theo, dragging the ax behind him and raised it to strike.

Theo tried to roll off the dais, but Cutter stopped in mid-strike and kicked him off. He hit the ground hard and rolled across the grass, stunned. Cutter was on top of him in an instant, with one hand on Theo's neck, and the ax raised in the other.

"It's over, bear."

I've got to talk my way out.

"If you kill me, Stratus will be mad."

"What?!" Cutter stopped. "You're right. It would be much better to see His Grace rip the stuffing out of you himself."

He lifted Theo by the throat and inspected him.

Theo tried to think fast; he saw a torch burning on the dais. "Which way is Stratus's castle?" he asked.

Cutter turned and pointed east. "There."

"I don't believe you."

"Why would I care whether you believe me?"

"Why don't you cut down one of those trees so that I can see? I'd like to know where I'm going to die, that's all."

Still carrying Theo, Cutter growled and stomped toward the tree line. Theo reached over as they passed the dais, grabbed the torch and jammed it into Cutter's neck.

"Yowch!" Cutter dropped the Whatsamadoozle in the grass, and Theo snatched it.

"Tricked you. The Whatsamadoozle is mine, now," Theo said.

Cutter patted out the flames on his neck. "You're a conniving little cub. You're going to pay for that."

Cutter spread his wings, and their edges began to move like chainsaws and made a terrible grinding noise. He swiped, but Theo jumped out of the way. Then he ripped around and sawed ten trees in half.

"Teddy bear cutlet. Sounds delicious!"

Theo took off into the forest with Cutter on his tail. The dinosaur cut down trees left and right as he followed.

The Whatsamadoozle glowed in Theo's hand. He imagined it as a mallet, and it flashed. A magnificent mallet, three times his size but as light as a small stick, pulsed in his hand.

He swung around and smacked Cutter in the chest. The dinosaur fell back, his wings sawing through several trees as he tumbled. One of them fell on him, but he threw the tree off and ran after Theo faster than before.

"You won't get away, bear!"

The trees rustled and shuffled around them as they ran.

Not again.

Cutter was unfazed by the forest movement. "Some measly trees aren't going to stop me from having teddy bear shish kebabs." He leaped into the air, his bony feet stretched wide to land on Theo, but Theo turned the Whatsamadoozle into a shield with spikes. Cutter landed on it instead and yelled, jumping away. He reared his wings back and fired two slicers of blue energy at Theo. They looked powerful, and Theo didn't know if the shield would protect him.

The trees kept shuffling around, and Theo spied a low-hanging vine on a nearby tree. He turned the Whatsamadoozle into a whip, aimed it at the vine, and he sailed into the air just as the energy slicers whizzed by him. Cutter passed beneath him, his wings cutting the trees that suspended the vine, and Theo fell to the ground.

Cutter pivoted and laughed; he was standing in the way Theo needed to go.

Theo turned the Whatsamadoozle into a flamethrower and aimed it at Cutter, engulfing the dinosaur in flames. Cutter screamed and put his wings over his face, but when the flames subsided, Theo saw that the wings were glowing—the flames had strengthened them.

"Ha. Ha." Cutter slashed the ground and set it on fire, creating a ring of fire around them. His wings spun and their fiery grind was deafening.

"Time for bear cutlets."

Theo turned the Whatsamadoozle into a rocket, and he flew through the forest with Cutter close behind.

"Not even a rocket can stop me from getting you," Cutter said.

Theo guided the rocket higher, flying through the canopy and into the sky above the trees. He saw the edge of the forest, so he turned the Whatsamadoozle into a parachute and started drifting toward it.

Below, Theo could see trees collapsing as Cutter continued to look for him. Suddenly, two blue energy slicers flew up from the forest and honed in on him. He turned the Whatsamadoozle into a sword, and he slashed at the slicers. Each strike knocked the slicers away and kept him airborne for a moment longer. When the last slicer fell away, he turned the Whatsamadoozle back into a rocket and shot toward the forest's edge just before he fell through the canopy.

Suddenly, something grabbed him, pulled him into the darkness and slammed him to the ground.

Dazed, Theo looked into Cutter's snarling face. The dinosaur raised his wing to strike.

Theo turned the Whatsamadoozle into an ice scepter. He waved the scepter and sprayed a torrent of ice and snow at Cutter, freezing him in a block of ice. The blast was so strong that it also froze all the nearby trees in a thick sheet of ice.

The area grew quiet, and the ice settled and cracked as it hardened.

Theo ran as fast as he could until he exited the forest. He looked back, but all was still quiet.

I'd better get away before he thaws. Over the hill, the lights of the caravan blinked, and he made his way up the dirt path.

Theo strolled back to the camp, and he turned the Whatsamadoozle into a yo-yo. He swung it with every step, and it sent off glowing golden rays that danced around the clearing, brightening everything.

The toys, who were building platforms and pitching tents, clapped when they saw the light.

"Oh mein gott!" Heinrich cried, putting his hands on his head.

Theo turned the Whatsamadoozle into a golden ball and handed it to Heinrich. The strongman jumped up and down and squealed.

"There," Theo said. He looked at Lucinda as he spoke. "If anyone here had any reservations before, I dare you to doubt me now."

Heinrich quickly turned the Whatsamadoozle into a giant mallet and rested it on his shoulder. "I never doubted you for one moment. You're a brave bear. Now I can fulfill my duty as the strongman, and I can smack the bell. Ya!"

Theo jumped on a platform and threw his hands in the air. "Who else could benefit from my services? You're in the protection of a real Ursabrand now."

The toys gathered at the base of the platform and cheered.

"Now it's your turn to help me, Lucinda," Theo said.

"We still need your help," Lucinda said.

Theo jumped down from the platform and glared at her. "What? I did what you asked me to." He pointed at the moon. "I'm running out of time!"

Suddenly, Bethany screamed and pointed in the direction of the forest. A purple streak was quickly approaching. As it neared, there was the sound of grinding saws and maniacal laughter. —Cutter.

"Not again," Theo said, drawing his broken sword.

"You won't get away," the dinosaur cried. He was covered with vines and twigs. "What have we here? A festival? Oooooh! I'm going to dash you all to plush and laugh when Stratus tortures you!"

Heinrich ran to the front of the festival grounds and pointed the mallet at Cutter. "Stand down, you Jurassic ruffian, or I will give you the biggest ouchy of your life."

Cutter grinned and kept approaching.

Heinrich spun around rapidly until he and the mallet began to glow. When Cutter neared—POW!—Heinrich smacked him so hard that he arced into the sky and disappeared over the horizon.

"And stay away!" Heinrich said.

Theo sighed. "He won't give up."

Heinrich scanned the horizon and shook his head. "Perhaps. It appears that you have more journeying ahead of you. I hate to give up my Whatsamadoozle again after such a joyful reunion, but I think you may need it more than I do."

"This will come in handy," Theo said, turning the Whatsamadoozle into a golden sword.

As Theo admired the sword, the wind blew, carrying distant screams. Soft at first, they grew louder until they filled the air. They were goose bump-making screams, so loud that Theo felt them in his bones. They were children.

"What is that?" Theo asked.

Heinrich shook his head. "Don't ask, my little cub."

Shaggy trotted to Theo's side. "Stratus is infusing the children with nightmares. It happens several times each night. Try to think happy thoughts. You'll get used to it, Theo."

He knew that Grant's scream was mixed in with the other children's. Theo scowled at the castle and said, "I don't know how you could ever get used to this."

The bell tower chimed, and the screams stopped and faded into the night. Though they were gone, Theo could still hear them in his mind, and he didn't want to imagine what horrible things Stratus was doing. But he had to know.

"How can you sit here and listen to that every night?" Theo asked.

"Stop judging us," Lucinda said. "You have no right."

"I have every right. This is unacceptable."

"We still need our mascot," she said, ignoring him. "If you can rescue him, then I can help you. I promise."

Theo dug his foot into the ground and scowled. He looked over at Bethany, who was smiling and motioning for him to come over.

Lucinda scoffed and hovered away, and Bethany uppercut the air as Theo approached.

"I knew you'd come and see ol' Bethany."

"Tell me what you want."

"I want my Gasket back."

"Make another one."

"Make?" Bethany asked. She put her hands on her hips and

stared at Theo so hard that he stepped back. "You can't just up and make a baby dragon."

Theo's eyes widened.

"I found him in the forest many years ago," she said, tearing up. "He's my best bud! He's better than any horse, too. If I don't get him back, I don't know what I'll do."

"Where is he?"

Bethany pointed to a rolling hill. The lights of a small town flickered on the top. "Darn rival circus. They kidnapped him last night. I know for a fact that Andersen the Clown took him. We're the best caravan in the Stratusphere and he's jealous. Envy-green, I tell ya!"

"Who is he?"

"He's the one in charge, but he's a third-rate clown in a second-rate caravan, if you know what I mean." She spit on the ground. "He's a balding, no-good, polka-dot-wearing, make-upped joke of a toy whose shoes are as big as Conestoga wagons. Oooh, he makes me so livid. His dung heap circus wouldn't even attract a hungry fly!"

Theo looked at the small town and guessed that it would be a short walk.

"Gasket's probably so scared," Bethany said. A wave of tears appeared in her eyes. "I can't imagine all the evil things that Andersen is doing to him. I just can't. So what'll it be? Will you help me, Mister Ursabrand?"

"Why don't you go and rescue him?"

"They need me here at the caravan," Bethany said, patting her biceps. "Besides, if I walked into town, they'd know me straightaway."

"Fine. I'll help you."

Bethany uppercut the air again. "Go get 'em, sir! And if you see that clown Andersen, sock him on his noisy red nose and tell him it was from me."

4

FINDING GASKET

Theo crested a hill and stared at the sky. The moon was bright, and clouds covered it like fingers.

The town lay at the bottom of a foggy valley. A bell tower rose over the small skyline, and under it, the yellow lights of houses flickered. The town reminded Theo of the old European cities that he had seen in Shawn's textbooks. Fog shifted here and there, exposing bits of tile roofs and cobblestone streets. Behind the town was a circus ground that was submerged in shadows; he could make out a Ferris wheel, a funhouse, and a small midway.

He stood, staring at all the different buildings, wondering where Gasket could be.

A noise behind him interrupted his thoughts. A wagon approached, drawn by blue carousel ponies that neighed as if possessed. Theo couldn't see who was inside the wagon.

He rushed to hide in a bush before the wagon passed, but in his hurry he accidentally dropped his shield on the path.

CRACK! The front wheel of the wagon rolled over the shield. It shot up and broke one of the spokes, causing the wagon to slump.

Oops.

"What the blue bazooka was that?"

A clown jumped out of the wagon and looked around angrily. He wore a polka-dotted clown suit with balloon pants, and his huge clown shoes clacked with every step and sounded like they were full of water. He had a red nose, dark, red eyes, and a faded white face with paint peeling at the cheeks. His orange hair looked like cotton candy, and it was partially covered by a triangle cap with a fuzzy cotton ball at the top that bounced when he walked. His voice was stuffy, as if he had suffered from a cold his whole life.

The clown limped over to the wheel and plucked the wooden shield out.

"Rats."

Two other clowns jumped out. One was a short, round female in a striped shirt. She wore a long, flowery skirt that flowed under her as she waddled. The other was a male, tall and lanky, with a face that reminded Theo of a bass. His clown suit was one size too small for him, and his wrists and ankles showed. He had bony joints that looked as if they could come unhinged at any moment.

"What's up, boss?" the female clown asked.

Andersen the Clown gazed around the clearing. Seeing no one, he shrugged and hurled the shield as far as he could. "Stupid dead toys, leaving their parts everywhere. I can't go anywhere anymore without being impeded by one."

"Praise Stratus for this impediment," the tall clown said. "May there be more of them!"

Andersen smacked the tall clown on the head. "You're supposed to agree with me."

The tall clown rubbed his head, and the female clown pointed at him and laughed. "Yeah, you're an idiot, Ludwig. You're supposed to agree with the boss."

Andersen smacked her on the head. "I hate suck-ups."

The female clown's eyes watered, and she scrunched her face up as if about to cry.

The tall clown laughed at her. "Yeah, no one likes a suck-up, Verona."

Andersen snarled at Ludwig and raised his hand to smack him again, but decided not to. Instead, he blew a whistle, and a group of wind-up monkeys scurried from the wagon. "Get to work."

The monkeys produced a spare wheel from the wagon and began to install it.

"Let's get some practice time in while we wait," Andersen said. "Fall into formation."

Ludwig climbed onto Verona's shoulders and juggled three balls while Verona started tap dancing out of rhythm. They posed with their arms wide and said tiredly: "Ta-da."

"No, no, no, no!" Andersen said, stomping toward them. "How many times've I told you?" He held out his arms wide and put on his biggest smile. "It's ta-daaaah!"

Ludwig and Verona chimed in and tried to imitate Andersen, completely out of tune.

"Taaaaaaa . . ."

"Daaaaaa . . ."

Andersen hung his head. "We need a million more hours of practice if we're going to be the best circus in the Stratusphere."

"But don't forget, boss," Verona said. "Now that we got that baby dragon, we're gonna—"

Andersen smacked her on the head again. "I told you: we don't talk about that out in the open. Someone might hear you."

"Sorry, boss . . ."

"But if you must know," Andersen said, "Yeah, that thing IS going to make us the best. That stupid gypsy caravan thinks they can win with a cute little mascot, but not anymore."

"He's ours now." Ludwig said.

Andersen grinned. "It's about time you got agreeable. Hyuk hyuk."

"Stratus is going to reward us for sure when we present it to him—after our circus, of course," Verona said, closing her eyes with delight.

"Just remember," Andersen said, grabbing the two clowns by the necks and pulling them close, "you two hold the keys to our success."

The monkeys saluted; the new wheel was installed.

"Let's get outta here."

Andersen threw himself into the wagon, and Ludwig and Verona followed.

Theo leaped out of the bush and climbed onto the underside of the wagon as it passed. It was a bumpy ride into town, and his arms were tired when the wagon finally stopped in the town square near a bubbling fountain.

The three clowns hopped down.

"We'll practice again tomorrow," Andersen said, tying the horses to a trough. "And don't forget what I said about that thing earlier."

"To success!" Ludwig said, saluting proudly. "Thank god we've got the keys."

Andersen smacked him on the head.

"Sorry, boss . . ."

Verona and Ludwig walked off in different directions while Andersen started down a dark alley, burping the whole way.

I need a place to hide.

Theo ducked into a church, a wooden building with stained glass windows and a bell tower.

He crouched inside the misty sanctuary. It was small and cozy. In front of the empty pews stood an altar with several lit candles and pictures of deceased toys next to them. He looked at each of the photos and wondered how they died—probably at the hands of Andersen, since he was one of Stratus's henchmen. Even though the clown looked like a bumbling fool, he was probably very dangerous.

There were no side rooms in the church. Gasket wasn't there.

Theo entered the bell tower through a small door in the back of the sanctuary and climbed six flights of stairs to the top, where the bell swayed in the breeze.

No Gasket.

Across the plains, he could see the castle. If only he could storm inside! He saw Grant's face in his mind's eye and imagined all the terrible things that Stratus might be doing to him. The thoughts were too much. He leaned over the tower railing, scowling and internally kicking himself for not being able to fight Stratus off.

He sulked on the tower for a while before he realized he was wasting time.

He exited the church and snuck down several streets until he came to the town jail, a gray building with a cupola and missing bricks. There were bars over the windows and several steps leading up to the door, which was locked with a rusty padlock. Theo activated the Whatsamadoozle, turned it into a blowtorch, and burned the lock off the door.

He entered to find a baby dragon sleeping in a jail cell that could hardly contain him. He was at least three times Theo's size, with black scales, long whiskers, triangular ears, and a paunch.

"Found you."

Gasket opened his sad green eyes, and then closed them.

"I'm here to save you."

Gasket exhaled and nearly blew Theo across the room. He sighed and closed his eyes again.

He doesn't trust me.

Theo tried to open the cell, but it was locked with a heavy padlock. Next to the padlock, a security panel with a fingerprint scanner and a microphone were bolted to the wall.

They really don't want him to leave. But where do I find the keys?

He stared outside at the town that lay before him. He could see a mansion on a hill, a tavern, the circus grounds at the edge of town, and a bazaar.

"I'll go to the tavern first."

* * *

The tavern was a gingerbread house with frosted windows. A sign above the door read THE DUELING GLOCK-ENSPIELS.

Theo climbed on a barrel and looked inside. A bunch of toys were scattered around the wooden tables, laughing as they played board games, told jokes, and passed around sippy cups filled with apple juice. A band was on stage, and two elves were at the forefront playing glockenspiels, each trying to outplay the other as the crowd cheered them on.

In one corner, a group of blue halibut passed around candy cigarettes and coughed up clouds of chalk that made a clown at a nearby table sneeze.

The clown was Ludwig, sitting alone at his table and staring at his thumbs as if he'd had too much to drink. One of the fish said something to him, and he shot to his feet.

Theo cracked open the window so he could hear.

"You hellacious halibut," Ludwig said, pointing his finger. "No one in this bar has the right to insult me."

One of the fish looked nervous. "You should stop drinking, buddy."

Ludwig swiped his sippy cup off the table and downed it. "I love apple juice, and you aren't going to stop me from drinking it. I dare any of you rapscallions to challenge me in an insult duel. I'll give my left arm to anyone who can beat me!"

"Who cares about your left arm?"

"I'll have you know that it's quite valuable," Ludwig said, unattaching it from the joint. "It contains the key to something important."

When no one responded, he slapped one of the halibuts with his arm. "You're all too scared, eh?"

Theo focused on the arm; its fingers were big—almost the same size as the fingerprint shapes on the security panel at the jail.

I get it now.

He climbed into the tavern through the window. "I'll challenge you."

Ludwig whipped around. "Finally."

"What are the rules?" Theo asked.

Ludwig eyed Theo. "I've never seen you before."

"I'm just passing through—Praise Stratus!—and I couldn't resist your challenge."

"You really want to play?"

Theo nodded.

"Very well. Let the game begin!"

One of the halibuts whispered to Theo. "You have to sling the worst insult. The big baby at the front of the bar will be the judge. Good luck."

The bar went silent, and a giant baby doll in a diaper sitting on the tap clapped his hands and giggled.

Ludwig stepped forward and surveyed Theo. "I've been looking at you for the last two minutes, and you're despicable to my sight, you fur-bedazzled lump bucket!"

"What the heck did you just call me?"

"A fur-bedazzled lump bucket!" Ludwig said, enunciating every syllable.

The bar oohed and aahed.

"That was the worst insult I've ever heard."

One of the halibuts nudged Theo. "Retort. Hit him hard with an insult!"

"You're a bass-faced, tack-gargling belly wobbler!"

"I'm a bass-faced, tack-gargling belly wobbler? Arrgh," Ludwig growled. "That was pretty good, I'll admit."

The big baby giggled.

"Baby liked it," the halibut whispered to Theo. "Keep it up."

Ludwig scowled. "Well, you're a plushy glooby disaster!"

"I'd love to know what glooby means," Theo said, as the bar laughed with him. "You're a barnacle-eyed stinky butter stick!"

"Barnacle-eyed stinky butter stick, eh?" the halibut asked.

Everyone in the bar snickered.

"He said stinky . . ."

"Stinky! Heh heh."

"I can't believe he said that. So brave!"

Ludwig looked around at everyone whispering, and he threw his sippy cup to the floor. "Arrrgh!"

The big baby laughed so hard that he fell off the bar.

"We have a winner!" the halibut yelled, holding up Theo's hand.

"I want a rematch!" Ludwig said, stomping up and down.

"Give me your arm," Theo said.

"Keep dreaming, teddy!"

"I said give me your arm."

Ludwig laughed, but Theo moved quickly. He grabbed Ludwig's arm, yanked it off and hit him over the head with it.

"Thanks."

Ludwig tried to get up, but the big baby stomped over and sat on him.

"Baby doesn't like you," the halibut said.

Ludwig struggled under the baby and then groaned.

Theo plucked off Ludwig's pointer finger and threw the rest of the arm back at him. "Change of heart."

He left the bar as everyone cheered at him.

* * *

"One key down," Theo said, approaching the circus grounds.

The circus grounds were unkempt—weeds grew everywhere and the carnie stands were in disrepair. The funhouse, a huge purple box with an angry mouth painted on it, was in need of paint, and the building looked like it was going to fall over any minute.

Theo paused when he spotted Verona sitting on a stump near the funhouse and playing with a lighter.

"We're the keys to success," she said. "What was the password? Ooooh, I can't remember!"

She stood up and did a ballet pose—"Ta-duuuuuh . . ."—then lost her balance, fell off the stump and hit her head. "I just can't remember."

She pulled a slip of paper from her pocket and read it. "Oh, that's it! How could I forget? It's—oh yeah, I shouldn't say it out loud in case someone is listening."

I need to get that piece of paper.

Theo grabbed a rock and threw it. It thunked off the funhouse.

"Yeeep!" Verona shouted, jumping three feet into the air. "Who's there?"

The breeze blew and rustled some leaves. Verona sat on the stump chattering her teeth.

"L-Ludwig? That you? You know how I hate when you play tricks on me. You better not be hiding inside the funhouse with a handful of insects like last time. I hate insects!"

She pulled a flashlight from her pocket and approached the funhouse; Theo tip-toed behind her and turned the Whatsamadoozle into a giant claw. He aimed it at her pocket just as he stepped in a patch of dry weeds. They crackled, and Verona started to turn around.

"Who's there?"

Theo turned the Whatsamadoozle into a gigantic kissing cockroach. The roach was twice her size, and its shell was an ugly brown. It smooched its big red lips as it neared Verona. It was the strangest cockroach Theo had ever seen, but it worked.

"Stay away!"

The cockroach tried to kiss her, but she shrieked and ran into the funhouse.

"Why are you running?" Theo asked. "It just wants to kiss you."

He entered the cool darkness of the funhouse, and a recording of Andersen's voice played through a speaker in the ceiling.

"Hyuk hyuk, welcome to my funhouse! I hope you find it fun—if you ever escape, that is."

A laugh track played, followed by a series of horrendous screams. The screams faded into suspenseful music that played the same low note over and over with a timpani boom every few beats.

Theo ventured farther into the darkness until he reached a neon-green wall with three doors in the shape of clowns' mouths. One was tall, one was fat and wide, and another was an electric revolving door with the reflection of fire on the other side.

He heard Verona's voice on the other side of the wall.

"Come and get me, you dum-dum!"

Theo entered the revolving door, joining Verona on the other side in a hall of mirrors.

"You weren't supposed to find me," she said. She started to run, but Theo turned the Whatsamadoozle into the kissing cockroach again. It reflected on every mirror, filling the room with hundreds of roaches.

Verona shrieked and froze, too afraid to move.

Theo turned the cockroach into the giant claw again and picked her pockets. He pulled out a toilet, a matching coffee mug set, and a roll of pennies.

"How much do you have in your pockets?" Theo asked.

Still in shock from the cockroaches, Verona only shook her head.

Theo kept digging in her pockets, but he couldn't find the slip of paper.

"Tell me the password, or I'll send out the roach again."

"It's f-fanny pack!" Verona said. "Please, no!"

"Fanny pack, huh? Pretty creative."

He left the funhouse, hearing Verona's screams behind him.

"Someone help me! I'll never come out again!"

Theo chuckled to himself as he ripped up the slip of paper.

As he left the circus grounds, Theo saw a large mansion on a hill overlooking the town. It was German-looking, with a brick and half-timber exterior. He had never seen such a huge mansion before.

He snuck toward the manor and came to a wrought-iron gate blocking the way. Grabbing a barrel from the alley, he climbed on top of it and threw himself over the gate.

The front lawn was manicured, and there was a fountain

with a statue of a laughing clown's face; water streamed from its eyes, but it was smiling.

He snuck around the side of the mansion, peeking in the windows as he went. There was nothing of interest inside—just fancy rooms with expensive decorations.

As he rounded the side of the house, bright light and heat suddenly surrounded him. Theo found himself standing in a library stacked wall-to-wall with old books.

How did I get in?

He stepped back and saw that the rear exterior of the mansion was missing, exposing the rooms. Here and there, teddy bear butlers moved throughout, dusting, cleaning, spraying, and waxing.

It's a doll house.

He could hear Andersen in a bedroom on the second floor, snoring on his bed.

Theo entered the library again and listened at the door leading out. Hearing nothing on the other side, he opened it and snuck into the hallway. The shiny wood floor was slippery under his feet, and portraits of toys, painted in oil, hung unevenly along the walls. Beneath each portrait was a caption in plated gold.

One portrait showed a serious-looking futuristic robot with a star on his chest, crawler treads for feet, and a laser gun in both hands. The caption underneath the photo read (FORMER) MAYOR ROBO. A knife had been stuck in the painting where the robot's face was.

He saw another portrait of a jack-in-the-box with legs. Its caption read (FORMER) MAYOR JACK, and a knife was stuck in his face, too.

All down the hall were portraits of different mayors with knives stuck in their faces, except for one at the end of the hall—Andersen's.

In his portrait, Andersen stood against a black background with his arms folded like a gangster, half his face covered in shadow. Next to his picture hung a portrait of Stratus. Only his eyes were visible. The caption below read MAY HE LIVE FOREVER.

This place is creepy.

Theo climbed the stairs. Reaching the top, he heard a sound and hid behind a sculpture of a kazoo.

A portly teddy bear butler was waxing the floor by hand. He wore a black tuxedo with long coattails. He wasn't an Ursabrand, and Theo despised him on sight.

"Oh my," Oxley said. "I must have missed a spot."

He inspected the top of the stairs. A bit of mud marked the otherwise shiny floor.

That's from me.

"I must trace the source of this most unfortunate speck, lest the master chastise me."

He followed the trail of mud that led toward Theo, but Theo pushed over the sculpture and hit Oxley in the head, knocking him out. He dragged the butler into a nearby closet, shut the door, and wedged the kazoo against the door so the butler couldn't escape.

Andersen's room should be down the hall.

Theo crept down the hallway, and as he did, he heard snoring; it was so loud that it shook the portraits on the walls.

He opened the door to Andersen's room. The clown was sprawled across his bed. Snot hung from his nose, and it rose and fell with each snore.

Theo hid in the closet, thinking of his next move, when Andersen suddenly startled and burped in his sleep. A golden key flew out of his mouth and clattered across the floor.

"Darn it," Andersen said, swiping up the key. He held it

over his mouth like an anchovy and he swallowed it whole. Then he fell asleep again, snoring louder than before.

Great. How am I supposed to steal the key when he's keeping it in his stomach?

There was a key ring on the desk next to Andersen's bed, with several different shaped keys on it. Theo picked it off the desk and wrestled a bronze key off.

He crawled under the bed and waited for a huge snore. When Andersen sucked in air, Theo punched the bottom of the bed. The noise startled Andersen so badly that he burped the key onto the floor.

Theo grabbed a baseball that was under the bed and threw it in the direction of the door.

Andersen shot up and ran to the door. "Huh? What? Who?"

Theo snatched the real key off the floor and replaced it with the bronze key from the ring. Then he slipped under the bed again.

Andersen opened the door and looked out. Seeing no one, he yawned and grabbed the old key without even noticing the switch. He swallowed it and fell asleep again.

Theo snuck out of the mansion without being seen.

* * *

Theo returned to Gasket's cell, where the dragon was still sleeping.

He unlocked the padlock with Andersen's key. Then he used Ludwig's finger on the fingerprint scanner. It beeped and unlocked.

The microphone shot in front of his face and asked, "What's the password?"

"Fanny pack."

The cell door didn't open. A camera descended from the ceiling and scanned Theo. "You are not Andersen. Intruder alert."

Alarms sounded, and Gasket woke up, looking around nervously.

"Crap." Theo ran outside and hid in a barrel.

Within minutes, Andersen, Ludwig, and Verona hobbled up to the building.

"Who do you think it was, boss?" Verona asked. "You don't think it was the gypsy caravan, do you?"

Andersen glanced around the square. "Don't know. But let's move him, just to be sure."

They went into the jail and led Gasket out in chains. Andersen kicked him to spur him forward.

"C'mon," he growled.

Theo ran from behind them and leaped onto Gasket's neck. He turned the Whatsamadoozle into a sword and cut Gasket's chains.

Andersen raised his fist at the sight of Theo. "Hey!"

Theo whispered into Gasket's ear. "I know you don't believe me, but I'm here to save you. Bethany sent me."

Gasket perked up at the mention of Bethany.

"So you're the one sneaking around," Andersen said.

"Get out of our way," Theo said.

"You're pretty sneaky. Why are you running around with those gypsies? We could use someone like you."

"I don't have time for you. Fly, Gasket! Fly!"

Gasket nodded and flapped his wings furiously. He blew fire at the clowns and sent them running for cover. Then Gasket lifted off into the air and hovered as he gained his balance.

Gasket took to the sky and the town shrank below them.

"Good job, pal," Theo said. "I think we're safe now." He

pointed in the direction of the festival grounds, far in the distance, and Gasket flapped his wings.

A roar sounded behind them, and Theo looked back to see another dragon rising into the sky. It looked like Gasket, but it was red, and its eyes glowed orange. Andersen was riding the dragon, and next to him flew Ludwig and Verona, with propellers attached to their heads.

"You have to be kidding me," Theo said.

Gasket saw the clowns approaching and whimpered.

Andersen flew closer. "You aren't going to get away. I've got a dragon of my own. Let's go, Wheelie!"

"It's okay," Theo said, patting Gasket on the back. "Just listen to me and we'll get through this."

"Get 'em!" Andersen shouted.

Ludwig flew forward and caught up to Theo and Gasket.

"You're mine," the clown said, reaching for Gasket's tail.

"Swipe your tail, Gasket!" Theo cried.

POW! Ludwig flew backward, but he balanced himself just before entering freefall. He flew at Theo and Gasket faster than before, brandishing a knife.

Theo slanted his eyes and jumped off Gasket. He grabbed Ludwig, dragging him downward, and knocked the knife out of the clown's hand.

"What do you think you're doing?" Ludwig said, trying to fly upward. "You're going to kill us both!"

Theo punched Ludwig, but his paw bounced off the clown's face.

POW! Ludwig punched Theo back, and the blow stung.

In the distance, Verona set a hot stone into her slingshot and aimed it at Theo.

Ludwig reared back to punch again, but Theo dodged the punch and climbed onto the clown's shoulder.

POW! Verona's stone hit Ludwig in the face, sending him and Theo plummeting toward the ground.

Gasket swooped under Theo, who landed on the dragon's back, but Ludwig crashed into a meadow below.

"Good job, boy!" Theo said, patting Gasket on the back.

Gasket entered a jet stream, flapped once, and the wind took him. Andersen and Verona followed.

"You can't get rid of us that easily," Andersen said.

Verona shot a stone, but Gasket rolled out of the way.

"We've got to take her out," Theo said, turning Gasket in her direction.

Wheelie and Andersen hung back, and when Verona saw Theo heading for her, she shrieked and began to fly away.

"Where are you going?" Theo asked, smirking.

Theo chased Verona into a nearby cloud, where she disappeared into the misty fog.

"Slow down, Gasket," Theo said, and the dragon hovered in midair.

They heard Wheelie fly by the cloud on their right. The red dragon roared and they heard a freezing, crushing sound—the cloud was hardening around them.

"Wheelie blew ice into the cloud," Theo said. "If we get trapped, it'll be like being inside an ice cube."

Gasket rolled out of the cloud just before it turned into a large ice cube and fell toward the ground.

Outside the cloud, Verona was waiting for them with her slingshot aimed at Theo. She released a stone. WHACK! The stone hit Theo in the stomach, knocking the wind out of him. He fell off Gasket's back, but Gasket caught him again.

Ahead, Andersen and Wheelie were flying directly at them.

"Heh heh." Andersen flapped Wheelie's reins, and the dragon roared.

He wants to play chicken.

Theo patted Gasket and stared at Andersen, scowling. "Straight on, Gasket. Don't pull up."

Gasket looked back at Theo and whimpered.

"Trust me, pal."

As they neared each other, the clown's smirk faded.

The two dragons were seconds from a collision.

"Wait for it . . ." Theo said, not taking his eyes off Andersen.

Andersen screamed and steered Wheelie up at the last moment, avoiding impact. Wheelie roared, flapped his wings frantically, and Andersen fell off.

"Darn . . ."

Verona caught him and held him under the armpits.

"See, boss? I won't let you fall."

But they were falling. Verona's propeller couldn't support both of them.

"You idiot! We're falling!"

"Sorry, boss . . ."

Andersen reached up, grabbed Verona's propeller and put it on his head. He kicked her away and she plummeted, screaming and crying the whole way down.

"Completely useless," Andersen said, landing on Wheelie. He threw the propeller away. "It's so hard to find good help anymore. I'll have to get rid of you myself."

Andersen tapped on Wheelie's neck. "Freeze them."

Wheelie blew a shot of icy breath toward Theo and Gasket.

Gasket looked back and blew fire. It met with the ice, creating a sparkling, spiky sculpture that hung in the sky for a moment.

Wheelie smacked the ice ball with his tail, sending it flying toward Theo and Gasket.

POW! Gasket sent the ice ball back toward Andersen with his tail.

POW! Wheelie sent the ball back toward Gasket.

The ball shot back and forth between them, growing smaller with each hit until it was the size of a volleyball. Theo caught the ball and threw it at Andersen's head.

Andersen fell off Wheelie and landed in a meadow below.

"Ugh . . ."

Wheelie landed and licked him, but he pushed the dragon away.

"Leave the caravan alone," Theo yelled. "Or you'll regret it."

Theo aimed Gasket toward the caravan grounds and they flew away.

5

THE FISH ON THE MOUNTAIN

Gasket landed in a valley at the base of a small mountain. The mountain was gray with rocks and bushes all over, and there was a wooden lodge at the summit.

"That's his home," Lucinda said.

"Then let's fly up there," Theo said. "Walking will waste more time."

Instead, Lucinda started up the winding path that led up the side of the mountain. "No. We walk. You'll see why."

Theo followed her reluctantly, with Gasket shuffling behind on foot.

"Why are we here?" Theo asked.

"Because my friend can help us get into the castle," Lucinda said.

As they climbed, a patch of golden brambles sprouted up before them and stretched the whole length of the trail.

"Where did those come from?" Theo asked.

Lucinda snatched the Whatsamadoozle from him, turned it into a giant saw, and cut her way through.

They were almost to the top of the mountain when the

bramble patch ended, and a purple tiger blocked their way. It breathed fire as it stalked toward them.

Lucinda returned the Whatsamadoozle to Theo, her hands glowing. Theo turned the Whatsamadoozle into a mallet, and Gasket roared and blew fire.

"Why do I get the feeling that this mysterious toy doesn't want to be found?" Theo asked.

"If you had listened to me instead of talking about yourself, then I would have told you."

The tiger leaped, but Theo knocked it away with the mallet. It rolled to its feet and charged. Theo swung again, but the tiger swiped the mallet out of his hand. It was about to slash when Lucinda's paws glowed even brighter. She hit the tiger with a dream blast, knocking it away.

Gasket blew fire at the tiger, and it finally turned and retreated up the mountain.

Lucinda petted Gasket. "Great teamwork, boy."

They started up the mountain again. The lodge had just come into sight when they heard more growling. The tiger had returned, and he'd been joined by three others. The four tigers stalked toward them, grinning and growling.

"Get out of our way," Lucinda said.

"Looks like we're in for a tough fight," Theo said, swinging the mallet in a circle.

"Stop," said a voice.

The tigers stopped and sat down obediently.

A blue catfish with big lips, large black eyes, and a deep frown on his face glowered from the doorway. He leaned on a cane, and he wore a brown, fish-scale sweater.

"That's enough."

The old fish squinted at Theo, Lucinda, and Gasket, and then he smiled. "Lucinda, my dear! I didn't know it was you."

He stuck his cane in the ground, and a magical wave rippled

over the mountain. The tigers disappeared, and an invisible force field around the lodge blinked purple and then faded away.

"So that's why we couldn't fly up here," Theo said. "He would have knocked us out of the sky."

Lucinda shook the old fish's hand. "It's good to see you again, Jiskyl."

"Pardon my paranoia," Jiskyl said, eyeing Theo, "I didn't recognize the other one."

"He's with me."

"You can't trust anyone in this place," Jiskyl said. "Not too long ago, a baby doll wandered up here—said she was scared. I was foolish enough to invite her in for a meal. She was one of Stratus's pawns, and she nearly killed me! I've been cautious ever since. Come inside. Are you two hungry?"

* * *

Jiskyl's lodge was cozy, decorated with photographs of friends on the walls and magical trinkets on shelves. A fireplace glowed warmly, and a large circular window overlooked the starry valley.

They sat by the fireplace, drinking hot chocolate. Theo and Lucinda sat on beanbags while Gasket curled up by the fire.

Jiskyl rocked in a rocking chair. "So, why are you here?"

"We need to get into the castle," Lucinda said.

Jiskyl nearly jumped out of his chair. "The castle! You don't remember what happened last time?"

"Stratus has Theo's owner."

"So you're racing to beat sunrise. The old desperate shuffle, eh? Why should I help you, Theo?"

"Because Grant's life depends on it," Theo said.

"And what about the festival, Lucinda?"

Lucinda put her hand on her heart. "Still scheduled."

"Are you going to help me or what?" Theo asked. "The moon's going to change again soon, and I need to know if I've wasted my time."

Jiskyl frowned at him. "Maybe you are wasting your time. You sound like one of Stratus's toys. Pushy. Aggressive. Always wanting something in return for anything you do."

"How dare you compare me to—"

"It's okay," Lucinda said, holding Theo back. She turned back to Jiskyl with a sad look. "He's really attached to his owner."

"Weren't we all?" Jiskyl asked. "But let me ask you, bear—what's going to happen to you after your pal grows up, hmm? Ever thought about that? What's next for you?"

Theo puffed. "That's a ridiculous question. Grant will always need me."

"Until the day he doesn't. You toys from the other side are sad. You come in here thinking that you can save this world, that you can return home as if nothing has changed." He stared out at the moon. "Toys like you never return home. They end up trapped here—not by Stratus, but by their own foolish dreams."

Silence fell over the room, and Theo thought it best not to speak. Jiskyl turned around and spoke softly. "I don't like you. I don't trust you. You're selfish, just like Stratus's pawns. The only reason I'm helping you is because of Lucinda."

Lucinda hung her head. "But—"

"Stop. I owe you, and you know it. If it hadn't been for you, he—"

Lucinda stopped him and hovered away. "But I still couldn't save him. I failed him."

Theo was confused. Who are they talking about?

"But you tried," Jiskyl said. "And that's more than I can say for all the other toys here. No one is courageous enough to challenge Stratus anymore." He focused on Theo and stared at him intensely. "Maybe you will succeed, Theo; maybe you won't. Maybe Stratus will find us and rip us all to shreds to set an example for the other toys, just for helping you. I don't care anymore. I haven't had an owner for decades. I have no attachments—just my love for living, which doesn't mean much anymore in this horrible place. I've got nothing to lose. Do you?"

"I have everything to lose," Theo said.

"Then you must make Lucinda's festival successful. If you do that, I promise to help you."

"Why do you care about this stupid festival?"

"What!" Jiskyl yelled. "I wouldn't expect a fresh toy like you from the other side to understand. But I'll answer your question, anyway: The festival is the only time we can gather to honor our lost friends. It's what he would have wanted."

"Who?" Theo asked. Who is this mysterious friend?

Lucinda changed the topic. "How are we going to get inside the castle?"

Jiskyl walked over to a desk and pulled out one of the drawers. It was full of glowing, magical items.

"Jiskyl!" Lucinda cried. "Please tell me you didn't steal those from the castle."

The old fish laughed impishly. "Why do you think my magic is so strong, my dear? Besides, if Stratus wanted to kill me, he would have done it by now. Now, what was I looking for? No, not a magic wand. Too typical. A crystal? No, too obscure. Aha!"

He pulled out a small coin bag. It jingled and jangled when he shook it. He opened it, and a white light lit up his face. "Take this. You can have the whole bag. You'll need it later, but don't go running off to the castle just yet. I still have to develop a plan. But I know that these coins will help somehow. I think."

"You think?" Theo asked, rummaging through the bag.

"There are a ton of coins in this purse, and they're all marked differently."

"A thank-you would be nice. You're as ungrateful as a toddler."

"But how am I going to get inside the castle?" Theo asked.

"Give me some time to investigate. I'll meet you at the festival. And Theo—don't forget your part of the deal. I'm putting a great amount of trust in you. Don't screw it up!"

Theo tied the coin purse and harrumphed.

Jiskyl leaned on his cane and gazed over the valley pensively as Theo, Lucinda, and Gasket headed back down the trail.

6

WAG THE DOG

When they returned to the festival grounds, Theo spent half an hour pitching a tent. He couldn't stop thinking about Jiskyl; he resented the way the old fish had treated him.

He spoke to me like I was an immature brat. I'm not your average toy. I don't care about this festival. Saving Grant is more important. Why can't he understand that a boy's life is more important than any toy's need?

He glanced around the festival grounds, where everyone was working hard. Heinrich plugged in a cable and lit up the midway, and everyone cheered. He flexed his muscles and shouted, "We're almost done!"

Bethany clapped and caught Theo's eye. She motioned for him to come over and celebrate with them, but he kept pitching the tent.

"Aw, c'mon, buddy. We couldn't have done this without ya!"

"You are an eternal friend of our festival," Heinrich said.

Theo ignored them and hammered in another nail.

I don't belong here. They're nice toys, but I'm not here to make friends. An Ursabrand cannot become attached to anything other than his owner. I can save Grant without their help. Now that I've got the Whatsamadoozle, I'm unstoppable. I don't need that old fish. Or Lucinda.

The toys moved to another area, out of sight, and his thoughts raced. He kicked a nail and decided that he didn't want to be at the festival anymore; he didn't want to be near the caravan. As nice as they were, every minute he spent with them diminished his chance of rescuing Grant. He felt bad, but he had learned how to hide his emotions—an Ursabrand had to. He accepted that sometimes, in order to protect the ones you love, you had to push friends away. The same thing had happened with Grant's other toys at home; they hardly spoke to him anymore. It was sad, but loneliness was the price that he gladly paid for Grant's life.

Theo took to the shadows, and he had almost sneaked away for good when Shaggy stopped him.

The dog stood looking at him with his head cocked. "You're leaving?"

"It's nothing personal, Shaggy."

Shaggy trotted up to him. "Pardon my interruption, Theo. But I have information that you will find valuable. It's about the castle." He wagged his tail and led Theo behind a wagon. When they were in the safety of shadows, with the moonlight between them, Shaggy spoke in his robotic voice.

"You want to get into the castle, right?" he asked.

Theo nodded.

"There's an entrance that no one knows about. I was passing through the Dream Marshes many years ago, and I got lost and ended up at the castle wall. There was a big crack in it, and it led to the courtyard. I still have the location programmed in my GPS coordinates, and I can take you there."

"Why are you helping me?" Theo asked.

"I want revenge against Stratus, too. He took my owner,

Gregory, and I want to save him. It's why I kept the location in my memory." He circled Theo, wagging his tail wildly. "You're the only toy I've ever met in the Stratusphere who has courage. I know that you can defeat Stratus and save us all."

"It's about time someone recognized my ability," Theo said.

"What do you say? Let's get out of here and have a real adventure."

"How much time will it take?"

"We can make it to the castle before the moon changes."

"That should give me plenty of time to defeat Stratus."

He thought of Jiskyl and Lucinda again, and anger bubbled in his stomach. He sheathed the Whatsamadoozle and followed Shaggy away from the festival.

They stood on the edge of a vast wetland that stretched for a great distance until it reached the castle. The air was sultry, with smoke rising out of turbid pink, purple, and green pools.

"So these are the Dream Marshes," Theo said. "Why do they look so different from the rest of the Stratusphere?"

"They're the source of Stratus's power," Shaggy said. "It's where he stores all of his nightmares."

"This looks dangerous, Shaggy."

"It's only dangerous if you don't know where you're going," Shaggy said, sniffing the air.

Theo followed Shaggy in, and they trudged through the marsh for a while. The pools of water bubbled and popped as they passed.

"Why are they bubbling?" Theo asked.

"It happens as travelers pass," Shaggy said. "Try not to think too much. The water can sense your mood and reflect your memories."

Theo looked around him and felt unsettled. He stayed close to Shaggy, who kept moving, guided by his GPS.

Unwittingly, Theo stepped into a pink puddle, and the marsh swirled around him.

Shaggy was gone.

"Shaggy!" he cried, but there was no response.

Theo ran and ran. He thought he saw Shaggy ahead and hurried toward him. But then Shaggy was farther away.

"Shaggy!" he called.

"Theo!" Shaggy called back. "Where are you?"

Theo saw Shaggy again, swirling in the distance. When he finally caught up to him, the dog was standing near a green pool.

"We've got to get out of here," Theo said. He stumbled, and the marsh swirled around him again.

A wooden cage fell out of the sky and landed over Theo. Everything stopped swirling, and Theo saw Shaggy floating in front of the cage; his legs had turned into hover jets and his eyes pulsed violently.

"Get me out of here," Theo said. He put his hands around the cage bars, but he couldn't escape.

"Silly bear. You should never have followed me in here."

Theo's eyes widened. "You betrayed me."

"Stratus will reward me," Shaggy said, sticking out his tongue. "I'll be his number one toy now."

"Why are you working for him? He'll just use you."

Shaggy sped around the cage, laughing. Theo circled the cage in reverse. He didn't dare turn his back to the dog.

"My dream is to rule a town one day."

"But what about your owner?"

Shaggy shrugged. "He probably died a long time ago. It's of no importance to me."

"The caravan—they trusted you."

"And now I can prove that they've conspired with you to overthrow Stratus. Soon, my allies will invade the festival grounds and detain them. They will die agonizing deaths, and it will be glorious."

The Whatsamadoozle had fallen out of Theo's sheath when the cage fell over him, and it was lying on the ground near him. He inched toward it.

"Why won't you join us?" Shaggy said. "You could rank even higher than me, Theo. You could have your own entourage, your own city, your own life back. No children to obey, no parents to worry about, no pets to chew on your parts at night. This is all Stratus wants for you. If you could only—"

Theo snatched the Whatsamadoozle, turned it into a buzz saw, and cut his way out of the cage. Then he shifted it into a battering ram and smashed into Shaggy, knocking him into a nearby puddle of nightmares.

"No!" Shaggy cried.

Theo turned the Whatsamadoozle into a golden sword and prepared to strike. "You betrayed me, and now you'll face the consequence of your actions."

Shaggy growled. He hovered into the air, and his body began to glow. A door on each of his shoulder pads opened, and he shot two fiery missiles at Theo. Theo jumped out of the way, and the missiles exploded against the ground.

A fan descended from Shaggy's stomach and blew marsh water into Theo's face.

"Marsh water won't defeat me," Theo said, running at Shaggy. But after a few steps, a strange feeling seized him and he lost all sense of direction. His head throbbed so badly that he dropped the sword.

"It's not just water." Shaggy disappeared, and suddenly Theo was in a factory where many hooks hung above him. Pistons were pumping, saws grinding, vats bubbling. Conveyor belts crisscrossed the room. Overhead, the moon shone through a skylight.

Shawn was sitting on a conveyor belt. He wore his red hoodie, with the hood over his head.

"Shawn?" Theo ran toward him. As he got closer, he realized that Shawn was moving across the room. He was crying, his tears pooling underneath him on the conveyor belt.

"Hold on, buddy," Theo said, but then he saw Shawn again —this time on another belt. This Shawn was quiet, sitting with his hands in his pockets and his knees tucked against his chest.

"Two Shawns?" Theo said, stopping.

Another Shawn passed by on a different conveyor belt; this one was screaming hysterically, as if he were being tortured by an unseen ghost. The screams hurt Theo and he didn't know what to do.

I can't think straight. This can't be real . . . I have to save him!

Before Theo could react again, he saw Shaggy hovering on a catwalk above. Shaggy pulled a lever, and the conveyor belts sped up—running toward a metal mouth in the wall that chomped incessantly.

"Shawn is going to die," Shaggy said. "You better save him—if you can pick the right one, that is." The conveyor belts picked up speed.

"No!" Theo cried.

Theo knew that he might only have one chance. He leaped and pulled the crying Shawn off the conveyor belt. When they landed on the ground, Shawn was gone, and Theo felt something carrying him by the arm.

He was in Shawn's bedroom. There was a crib with a mobile of stars. The toy box that he had known all his life was in the middle of the room on a rug, but there were no toys in it yet. It was sunrise, and light shone into the room in soft angles.

I remember this. Shawn was a baby on this day.

The person carrying him stopped moving and brought him higher. It was Mom. She looked so young. Her hair was pulled back in a long ponytail, and she wore a flowery dress. What he remembered most about her during these days was her warmth; he could feel it again, and he felt so comfortable.

"Well, Mr. Theo, it's time to meet your best friend," she said. She turned him so that he could see baby Shawn wriggling and cooing in a blue blanket.

She set him next to Shawn and left them alone.

Theo lay with Shawn and watched the sunlight flowing through the window.

"I failed you, old pal," Theo said.

Shawn cooed and grabbed Theo's nose.

"You don't hate me anymore?"

Baby Shawn began to cry.

"No, I'm sorry. Don't cry—"

Now Shawn was crying uncontrollably, and every gasp hurt Theo's heart.

"It's going to be okay. I won't let anything hurt you."

Shawn kept crying, louder and louder. It was deafening, and it was driving Theo crazy.

He stuffed a pacifier in Shawn's mouth. Shawn stopped, sucked the pacifier, then spit it into Theo's face and cried louder than before.

I forgot. He always hated pacifiers. Maybe I can tell a joke.

"Once, there was a donkey," Theo started, but Shawn kept crying. "The donkey walked into a daycare looking for his owner, and, and—"

Shawn kept crying.

Theo took a blanket, held it to his face, and blew into it with all his might, making it billow.

Shawn saw this and laughed. Theo laughed with him, and then Shawn started to cry again.

"Oh no . . ."

Shawn stopped crying and looked at Theo with faint amusement.

"Good," Theo said. Theo turned on the mobile, and the stars and moon began to whir.

One of the baby's eyes glowed red for a moment, and Theo stepped back.

"Something's wrong. You're not—"

Suddenly, Baby Shawn stood up on two feet and holding a roaring chainsaw. Theo rolled away, and his surroundings morphed back into the factory. The crib turned into a conveyor belt; Theo was on top of it, and he was seconds away from the chomping mouth. He jumped off just in time.

All the machinery in the room stopped.

Shaggy barked from above. "I hate it when the system malfunctions." He raced to a security panel on the other side of the factory.

Meanwhile, the other Shawns were stuck on the conveyor belt in front of the mouth; it hadn't eaten them yet.

Theo grabbed the quiet Shawn off the conveyor belt and they rolled across the floor.

Shawn disappeared, and Theo was back at home, lying on the kitchen table while Mom and Dad paced around the kitchen.

"Where do you think he could be?" Mom asked.

"He's got to be around the neighborhood somewhere," Dad said.

Theo wanted to move, but he couldn't as long as Mom and Dad were in the room. A policeman knocked on the back door.

Theo remembered. *No. I don't want to relive this day.*

Mom, Dad, and the officer went into the living room to talk.

Theo jumped off the table and ran through the hall, past puppy Amos who was sleeping in his bed, and upstairs into Shawn's bedroom, which was filled with toys.

Shawn wasn't there.

"I'm too late."

He saw a portal glowing under the bed—the same portal that had appeared after Grant had been abducted.

"This was my fault," Theo said. "And now I've got a second chance to fix it."

He ran toward the portal, but it imploded just before he reached it. The explosion knocked him out of the bedroom, downstairs, and onto the sofa where Mom and Dad were talking to the officer.

"When was the last time you saw your son?" the officer asked, scribbling on his notepad.

"Last night," Mom said. She was in tears, and Dad put his arm around her.

"How old is he?"

"Nine."

"Do you have any enemies?" the officer said.

Dad shook his head.

"It's been forty-eight hours, so that's strange. Kids usually come back home on their own by this time. And you're sure no one came through the window?"

"It's locked from the inside," Mom said, sobbing.

The officer bunched his lips and picked up Theo by his neck. "This his?"

Mom and Dad nodded.

"What a terrible teddy bear," the officer said, smirking at Theo. "He couldn't even protect a nine-year-old. Ha ha ha . . ."

Theo tried to free himself from the officer's grip, but he couldn't.

Now Mom and Dad were laughing with the officer. Dad

was slapping his knee, and Mom was laughing hysterically, with sad tears still streaming down her cheeks.

"I think you need to throw this guy in the trash!" the officer said.

Theo swiped at the officer but couldn't reach. Meanwhile, the chokehold grew tighter.

"You don't know the whole story," Theo said, gasping. "I—"

"I do know the whole story," the officer said, carrying him past the big TV and stereo and toward the garbage disposal in the kitchen. "You failed your oath as an Ursabrand. And now you will face the consequences of your failure."

"No—"

Theo grabbed the remote control off the entertainment center and hit the officer in the eye; the officer let go of Theo and screamed. His body warped into Shaggy, who growled and flew away, out of reach.

They were back in the factory, and Theo was on top of a conveyor belt again and even closer to the chomping mouth. He jumped off just in time.

Suddenly, all the machinery in the room stopped again.

Shaggy growled. "I really need to reboot this factory."

The screaming Shawn hadn't been eaten yet. Theo pulled him off the conveyor belt and they crashed to the ground.

Shawn disappeared; Theo was in Shawn's bedroom. It was dark, and moonlight was shining through the window.

Theo looked around. I remember this night.

A portal appeared under the bed, and Shawn climbed from it, gasping and heaving. He looked as if he had been attacked; he was sweating and his eyes were wild and unfocused.

He was nine when this happened, the same age as Grant now.

Shawn crawled forward and screamed.

"It's okay, pal," Theo said, patting Shawn on the back. "You're safe from Stratus now. You're going to be okay."

Shawn pushed him away and kept screaming.

Quick footsteps pattered outside the door, and Mom and Dad rushed into the room. Seeing Shawn on the floor, they took him into their arms, crying with joy and sadness.

The portal closed quietly under the bed.

Theo shrank into the closet as Mom tried to console Shawn.

"What happened?" she asked.

But Shawn kept screaming.

"Honey, you have to tell me what happened," Mom said, tears in her eyes.

Shawn looked back at the bed where the portal had been and kept yelling.

Dad got on his knees and looked under the bed but saw nothing but socks. He checked the window—he had put tape there to detect intruders—but it was shut fast. He was baffled. "I don't know where he came from, or how he got back." He stood staring at the window. Young Grant was in his arms, and when he sensed Dad's uncertainty, Grant began to cry.

"He was in the Stratusphere," Theo said, even though Mom and Dad couldn't hear him. "And somehow, he escaped. I don't know how. But he's safe now, and I promise that this will never happen again."

Suddenly several shadowy hands appeared from under the bed and positioned themselves to grab Mom and Dad, Shawn, and Grant.

"No!" Theo cried. He charged at one of the hands, but it smacked him away. The hands rose into the air and converged into a giant fist that came down toward Theo. He rolled away, and the surroundings changed back to the factory.

The giant hand was a giant piston; Theo was on a conveyor

belt, once again seconds away from the chomping maw. He jumped off before it ate him.

"Why won't you die?" Shaggy growled.

The factory bubbled and popped around Theo. The marsh blinked into view, and then the factory appeared again. The changing scenery gave Theo a headache.

The illusions are wearing off. I'll create an illusion for him.

He clutched his heart and cried, "Shawn! Shawn!" He pretended to wander around the factory. He felt the Whatsamadoozle on his waist—Shaggy hadn't taken it.

Meanwhile, Shaggy hovered closer, his tongue a blasting blowtorch of flames.

The Dream Marshes blinked back into sight and Theo saw an iridescent pond next to his foot.

A little closer . . .

"Time to die," Shaggy whispered.

Theo activated the Whatsamadoozle, turned it into a bucket, scooped up water and splashed it in Shaggy's face.

"No—"

Shaggy's body sparked. "You've short-circuited me—"

That was his last coherent thought. The dog paused and looked into the distance, squinting. "Gregory?"

Smoke rose from the dog's shoulders. He barked, but no sound came out. He ran away, crying out for Gregory. "Don't run. I've waited for you. I need you!"

One of Shaggy's legs stopped working, but that didn't stop him. He moved deeper into the shadows of the marsh, screaming and whimpering. "Gregory . . ."

Another leg stopped and Shaggy fell face-first. He called out for Gregory again; his voice rose five octaves, sank ten octaves, then his body exploded.

"What a shame," Theo said, standing over the dog's body. "I wish it didn't have to end this way."

But he couldn't stop thinking about Shawn. The memories were so vivid he could still imagine himself there. A wave of anxiety fell over him and his heart felt heavy.

Was that real? No, it couldn't have been. Everything is so weird here, I can't know for sure. I've got to get out of here.

And then he remembered the caravan.

I've got to warn them before it's too late.

He turned the Whatsamadoozle into a propeller and flew out of the marsh.

The Dream Marshes fell away, and the farther Theo flew, the less heavy his heart felt, though he would never be able to forget what he had seen. He focused on the sky and hoped that he could get back to the festival grounds to save Lucinda and the caravan.

He passed over a rocky plateau lined with a trail of colorful, painted squares that snaked all over. It was a strange-looking place; if he didn't know any better, he'd say it looked like a board game . . .

Something knocked him out of the sky, and he landed on a green square with START written on it. He stood up and tried to fly away, but an invisible force bound his feet. He couldn't move.

"What the—"

A small flying saucer loomed over him. Maniacal laughter came from inside while cheesy music played from a speaker on the bottom.

"Let me out of here!" Theo cried.

The spaceship danced in the air. "Welcome, challenger. You are the first—and last—contestant in the greatest board game of all time!"

7

ALIENS & OTHER INCONVENIENCES

The saucer rocked from side to side and a door on top opened. A big-headed, green alien with black eyes and a stitched-up slit over his mouth popped out. He rubbed his head, which had a huge, peanut-shaped hump in the back. The nerves on the hump were outside his skin, glistening like the pathways on a silicon chip, and the skin on his long, spindly arms looked oily. When he spoke, his voice came from the speaker of the flying saucer, not his mouth. His voice was ethereal and multi-layered, as if five of him were speaking at the same time.

"Darn door. It gets jammed every time."

He shifted in his seat and hovered the saucer around Theo. "How do you like my creation? I, Braindon, of the Tarapsha'Na-Xinaxhat Colony, am its mastermind. It took me forty-three million, six hundred thousand, five hundred twenty-nine minutes and nineteen seconds to build. I had to import the selerium that powers the board from distant galaxies, and I spent many decades in my laboratory concocting the right formula to get the board to light up." His eyes glowed as he gestured across the board proudly. "Oh, the brain power it took! Thank goodness I have a big brain, because the square root of the area was not conducive to the mass of the illusions that Stratus gave me—"

"Shut up and speak English," Theo said.

Braindon balled his fists and the saucer shook. "How dare you interrupt me? I've never been able to practice my speech to anyone before. Don't ruin my moment of fame."

Theo turned the Whatsamadoozle into a bow and arrow. "Let me out of here."

Braindon shook so hard his skull glowed. "You ungrateful teddy bear. I was going to explain the rules of the game to you, but now you don't deserve to hear them."

"Rules?"

"Now you'll never know what they are. The only way I'm going to let you out is if you play."

Theo shot an arrow, but it passed through the saucer without seeming to even touch it.

Braindon paused; he closed his eyes and held up his hands. "What's that? Yes, I hear you, brothers. Speak to me. Om . . . Ooooom . . ." He waved his hands as if he were doing tae kwon do. "Your message is clear. This teddy bear is trying to defy Stratus, and he must be stopped . . ."

"That's the most pathetic show I've ever seen. You knew that all along."

Braindon opened his eyes. "So what? I was confirming my suspicions with the collective."

"What collective? You're a toy, not an alien."

"Nonsense. I am from the Tarapsha'NaXinaxhat Colony."

"And where exactly is that?"

"In the Cerulean Quadrant."

"Cerulean is a crayon color."

"How dare you relegate my home quadrant to a human design apparatus!" Braindon pulled out a remote control with a huge knob on it, and he turned the knob all the way to the right.

The remote control vibrated, and all the squares on the plateau pulsed.

A floating deck of cards appeared in front of Braindon and he placed his hand on it. "Maximum difficulty for you, teddy bear. It's time to begin the game."

Theo slid onto an empty green space. The square shimmered, and a purple monkey appeared. He was blindfolded and tied to a chair, and he was screaming. Blue dynamite sticks were strapped all over his body, and on his chest a touchscreen tablet blinked.

"Help me!" the monkey cried.

"What kind of challenge is this?" Theo asked, disgusted.

"An experiment," Braindon said. "I left my dissection tools back at the colony, so blowing up my subjects is the next best thing—that is, unless you can defuse the bomb."

"I'm going to die," the monkey said. "I'm going to diiiiie!"

"Shut up," Theo said. He bent over, inspecting the touchscreen on the monkey's chest, and the screen lit up with words.

There were so many of them that it was hard to remember them all. Then, just when Theo was starting to memorize them, the touchscreen shut off.

"Hey, that's not fair," Theo said.

"You're going to get us killed! You touched it wrong!"

"I didn't even touch it."

The monkey screamed again, and the touchscreen blinked on.

I can't remember the words anymore. It was a trick.

A quiz appeared on the screen, asking him to select three words that hadn't appeared on the touchscreen before. He answered, and to his surprise, his memory was better than he thought.

"Congratulations! Three out of three correct," the touchscreen said.

"Phew," the monkey said as the dynamite fell off him. "I'm out of here!"

He scampered across the plains and was gone.

"Well done," Braindon said, snarling. "You may proceed."

Again an unseen hand slid Theo down the board onto another square that lit up when he landed on it.

"Time for a new challenge," Braindon said.

He retreated into the saucer, and the ship divided into three units. They spun around so fast Theo couldn't follow them. Then they stopped, and he heard Braindon's laughter.

"Where am I? You only get one guess!"

Theo scanned the saucers—it would be a completely random choice.

"Left," Theo said.

The left and middle saucers exploded, and Braindon popped out of the right one.

"Failure," he said. "My game is better than I thought."

"That's because it's rigged," Theo said, readying himself for the next space.

He slid several spaces ahead, into a circle.

Braindon hovered over a black square. "Now we battle. You can either draw or attack each turn. The game ends when one of us is defeated."

Against his will, Theo slid onto a white square. He activated the Whatsamadoozle and turned it into a sword. "You're finally speaking a language I can understand."

I should draw to see what happens, first.

The square shimmered at Theo's feet, and he drew a card with a metal shield on it.

"A Shield Card," Braindon said.

A force field of selerium energy rose around Theo, preventing damage from the next attack.

"Give up now," Theo said.

Braindon snickered. "I knew you'd do that. But you shouldn't doubt the darkness. Well . . . nah. I don't think I'll draw."

ZEER! Braindon fired a laser at Theo, but the force field protected him and then disappeared.

Theo drew a card with a box of tissues on it. He waited for something to happen, but nothing did.

Braindon laughed. "A Tissue Card? Not good." He fired a laser at Theo, knocking him back.

Theo stood and screwed his eyes at Braindon. "Why haven't you drawn yet?"

Braindon harrumphed.

I'm not going to draw this time.

Theo slashed Braindon, making the saucer wobble.

Braindon drew a card with a box of tissues on it. Nothing happened. "I hate Tissue Cards."

Theo chuckled and drew a card with a clock on it. He moved at twice his normal speed and slashed Braindon two times.

"I prefer not to draw yet," Braindon said. He shot a laser at Theo, knocking him back.

Theo drew a card with a shadow cloud on it. He froze in place as dark energy swirled around him and squeezed him.

"How did you like that Shadow Card?" Braindon said, laughing. He fired another laser at Theo.

The shadows disappeared, and Theo drew a card with a ball of light on it.

"A Summon Card!" Braindon cried. "You weren't supposed to draw that."

The Whatsamadoozle glowed so brightly it filled the area with light. In an instant, Theo saw the faces of all the toys in the Stratusphere who had ever died, and they smiled at him before turning into white energy that flowed across the area in milky tendrils.

"That light—" Braindon said, shielding his eyes.

Theo pointed the Whatsamadoozle at Braindon, and the light surged into the spaceship. An explosion knocked Braindon out of the air. Then the light disappeared.

Theo slashed Braindon, and the saucer powered down. The alien groaned as the board game powered down, too.

"Now let me out of here," Theo said.

Braindon shook his fists. "It cannot be," he said. "It was supposed to be the perfect game. You shouldn't have won."

Theo felt the invisible hold on his legs disappear. He turned the Whatsamadoozle into a giant claw and grabbed the spaceship, slamming it several times until it broke into many pieces. Braindon tumbled out and lay on the ground, clutching dirt.

"I am a failure," he said, hanging his head. His voice was singular and thin now that his spaceship was broken. "I have allowed myself to believe lies. I was discarded by a child, and when I came here, I told myself that I could return to my place of origin. But it was never real. I am just a mere toy."

"I don't have time for a therapy session," Theo said, rolling his eyes. He started to walk away, but Braindon cried out to him.

"What will you do when it happens?"

"What are you talking about?"

"The moment you are jettisoned."

"I'll never be jettisoned."

"You are a smart toy—almost as smart as me," Braindon said. "But regardless of your potential, you will face the same fate."

Theo balled his fists. "Be quiet."

Braindon chuckled. "Your owner will discard you like trash. It will be gradual. First, you'll see that he doesn't pay attention to you, and you will gather dust. Then, many agonizing years later, a box will be your home, and you will end up here."

Theo turned the Whatsamadoozle into a mallet. "I told you to be quiet."

Braindon ignored him and continued. "And I want to be there the moment you have to decide between a lifetime of irrelevance or Stratus's grace."

"Never."

"Then you will wander this world, and he will torture you for eternity. Don't become trapped by your dreams, bear. Save yourself while you are still uninjured."

Theo screamed and hit Braindon on the head with the mallet, not stopping until the alien was unconscious.

He stood over Braindon, breathing hard. "You talk too much," he said.

Braindon's body disappeared, leaving the ruined spaceship on the ground.

The alien's words had hurt him, but he couldn't accept such a terrible prediction of his fate.

He didn't have time to dwell. He remembered the caravan, and he once again turned the Whatsamadoozle into a propeller and flew toward the festival grounds.

8

NO MORE FRIENDS

Theo landed in the middle of the festival grounds and looked around frantically.

No one was there. All the attractions were overturned and broken.

I'm too late.

He searched the area—the midway, where he could smell the fresh paint from the broken stands; the carousel, with its smashed mirrors; and the big top, its shredded canvas flapping in the wind.

Sadness welled up inside him as the reality set in. He turned the Whatsamadoozle into a mallet and smacked the rubble of a nearby booth.

"I let them down," he said, smashing the booth even further. "They were my friends. They were trying to help me, even if it was in their own strange way. They're going to suffer now because of me." He fell to his knees, panting. "First Shawn, then Grant, and now them. Why can't I protect anyone?"

A blast struck him in the back and he flew across the midway.

"Ow . . ."

Jiskyl, the old catfish, stepped from behind the big top and approached Theo, scowling.

"Imagine my surprise," Jiskyl said. "I came to see how the festival was coming along—the very festival that you, dear sir, agreed to make successful—and I looked around and found no one, except for you. You killed them!"

Theo jumped to his feet, but the Whatsamadoozle was lying on the ground near Jiskyl. The old fish picked it up and put it in his pocket. "You lied to me," he said as his hands glowed. "You killed good toys, the only good ones left in the Stratusphere."

"It's not what you think," Theo said. "It is my fault, but I didn't kill them."

"No more lies!" Jiskyl said, knocking Theo into a carny stand with another blast. "You may report to Stratus, but that ends now. I will destroy you just like you destroyed that booth a minute ago."

Theo's eyes widened. "You don't understand—"

Jiskyl's hands glowed again, and Theo knew he couldn't take another hit.

"Stop," Theo said, wheezing. "I want to find them."

"They're dead!"

"But did you see them die?"

"No, but it doesn't matter. You killed them!"

"But if you didn't see them, how do you know they're dead?"

"Well, where are they, then?"

There was silence between them, and out of the shadows of the night came a steamy whistle, soft and distant. Choo choo . . .

Jiskyl ran to the edge of the grounds and gasped. A set of railroad tracks glowed, pulsing rainbow colors. They stretched into the distance, through the valley and into the mountains toward the castle.

"If you're telling the truth," Jiskyl said, "they must be aboard that train, wherever it is. Who knows how long ago it left?"

Jiskyl returned the Whatsamadoozle, and Theo turned it into a propeller.

"I have to save them."

Jiskyl wrinkled his face at Theo. "I still don't trust you."

"I don't need your trust."

Theo took off into the sky and followed the tracks, leaving Jiskyl staring after him.

9

BIG TROUBLE ON THE LITTLE CHOO CHOO

Theo descended through the clouds toward a red train chugging down the tracks. The engine spouted a gray column of steam and pulled a passenger car, a freight car, and a caboose.

I don't know why, but I know they're there.

He landed on the caboose. The fields of the Stratusphere zoomed by as the train picked up speed. There was a cupola on the roof, and the car's windows were ajar. Theo peeked inside.

The caboose was sumptuously decorated, with brocaded wallpaper, a chandelier that jangled occasionally from the ceiling, and several mahogany booths.

At a table in the middle of the car, three clowns played cards. Ludwig and Verona were joined by a muscular clown with a barrel chest wearing a Hawaiian shirt with parrots painted on it. A toy cigar with a glowing tip protruded from his mouth, and his hands were the size of ham hocks.

Great. I thought I finished them off a long time ago.

"Lud, gimme your queens," the muscular clown said. His voice was croaky.

"Go fish," Ludwig said, giggling.

"Where are we headed, anyway?" the muscular clown asked, studying his hand of cards.

Verona drew a card from the deck. "To the castle. We're going to deliver these toys and take the reward. Weren't you paying attention to the boss, Beasley?"

"I was busy running this train. It's hard work—something you two ain't used to."

"Bless Shaggy's heart," Ludwig said. "If he hadn't led that annoying teddy bear away, we never would've been able to nab the caravan. Now we're gonna be rich."

"Yeah, I hated that bear," Verona said. "But who cares? Shaggy's probably killed him by now."

"Hopefully," Ludwig said. "Did you see the shape of his head? Ha ha, I could tell jokes about him all night!"

Theo scowled.

"His head was so small, it would have made a shrunken head jealous."

Verona rolled her eyes, and Beasley said, "Jesus."

Ludwig slapped the table. "Come on, that was kind of funny."

Beasley shook his head. "No offense, but that was crap."

"Why?"

Beasley stared at Ludwig, incredulous. "Here's what you should have said: 'His head was so little, it's a wonder he has a brain.' That's a better basis for a joke. You can build upon it. You can paint a picture for the audience, then maybe move on to his other body parts, or tell an anecdote to support your leading joke. It's Comedy 101, Lud. You can't use that shrunken head garbage—they'd laugh you out of the big top. But hey—not all of us can major in jokes."

"So you're telling me that you're the king of comedy now?"

"I wouldn't call myself the king, but I don't know what you'd call yourself."

"How dare you, you onion-headed poochyfud!"

Beasley held up his hand to shut Ludwig up. "You're lucky I don't knock you out of this caboose."

Ludwig ripped off his arm and swung it at Beasley. Beasley flipped over the table, but Verona jumped between them. "Aren't we supposed to be celebrating? If the boss catches us fighting, he'll disconnect the caboose!"

Theo suppressed a laugh. *Great idea.*

He crept to the front of the caboose and dropped between it and the next car, where the coupling was. He looked through the window; Ludwig, Verona, and Beasley were still arguing.

Theo turned the Whatsamadoozle into a mallet and smacked the coupling several times, but it wouldn't budge. Each smack made a chinking noise.

The clowns were so busy arguing that they didn't notice the sound, but Theo heard footsteps coming from the roof of the car in front of him. Peeping onto the roof, Theo saw another muscular clown. He wore thick metal boots, and he looked as if he could squash Theo if he stepped on him.

"Hey!"

I'm vulnerable down here.

Theo turned the Whatsamadoozle into a propeller, flew up, and landed on the roof.

"You're that teddy bear the boss talked about," the clown said.

Theo turned the Whatsamadoozle into an electric whip.

"He gave us orders to rip you apart," the clown said, lunging toward him.

Theo cracked the whip, and the clown jumped back and pulled out an orange pistol. He pulled the trigger, but instead of a bullet, a flag with the word OOPS popped out.

"Sounds right to me," Theo said.

The clown blushed.

CRACK! ZZZT!

Theo smacked him, and the whip shocked the clown out of his metal boots. He sailed into the air and crashed into a field as the train left him behind.

Theo kicked the boots over and said, "That was easy."

"What was that?" cried a voice.

It was Beasley, and he was climbing to the top of the car.

Theo turned the Whatsamadoozle into a boomerang and threw it toward the caboose; it flew far, and then curved upward and back toward him.

Beasley climbed up and pounded his fists. "I thought you were supposed to be dead."

Theo backed away, eyeing the boomerang.

"You're no match for me," Beasley said. He grabbed Theo by the neck and laughed, then dropped him when the boomerang hit him in the back of the head. Theo rolled out of the way as Beasley fell over the side of the train and landed in a field.

He caught the boomerang and looked down at the caboose. Ludwig and Verona weren't inside.

They're up to something.

He ran to the edge of the car and looked down; Ludwig and Verona were climbing the ladder, but they were shaking and their teeth were chattering.

"Not you again," Verona said.

Theo turned the Whatsamadoozle into a mallet and jumped into the air.

Ludwig and Verona screamed, dropped off the ladder, and shielded themselves under the canopy of the caboose. Instead of hitting them, Theo landed on the coupling and smashed it, disconnecting the caboose.

Ludwig and Verona jumped up and down angrily as the caboose rolled backward down a hill.

"That takes care of them," Theo said.

The train chugged on up the hill, and Theo made his way to the next car. When he reached the roof, he almost fell off the train in shock. The top of the car was exposed, and the freight car was filled with dead toys and toy parts. It looked as if they were freshly murdered. Many of their eyes were still open.

Theo felt nauseous at the sight of all the dead toys.

Another clown sat on the opposite edge of the car, dangling his legs off the side. He was reading a book.

Theo dove into the sea of toys, swam through, and peeked out at the other end near the clown.

He turned the Whatsamadoozle into a slingshot and aimed, but he let go just as the train hit a bump in the tracks. The rock shot past the clown's ear.

"What the—?"

Cursing, the clown whipped around, snatched Theo out of the toy pile, and threw him overboard.

Theo turned the Whatsamadoozle into a propeller just before he hit the ground and flew back toward the train. He landed on the car, turned the Whatsamadoozle into a giant fan, and blew the clown away.

Andersen needs better security guards.

The passenger car was next, and Theo climbed down to look through the back window. The car was luxurious like the caboose, with several booths in the front. In the middle, a giant cage held Lucinda, Heinrich, Bethany, and Gasket.

I knew I'd find you.

Theo disconnected the freight car behind him, and it rolled away. He turned around to enter the passenger car, and had just put his hand on the door when something told him to stop. He ducked and kept his eyes on the window.

Andersen entered the car from the opposite side, shoes clacking as he walked. He whistled and puffed a candy cigar.

"Gonna be rich," he sang. "Gonna be riiiiiich . . . dooby doo . . ."

"Quit yer lousy singin'," Bethany said.

"This is your last chance to join Stratus," Andersen said. "You really don't have to sacrifice your lives for that teddy bear. His Grace is still willing to accept you. Of course, I wouldn't be happy if you joined us because it would minimize my reward. I need it to build a new big top. But I'd be happy for you. I wouldn't have to pity you pathetic toys anymore. How horrible it must be to live like you do, on the fringe, moving from town to town because no one will accept you . . ."

Lucinda shot a dream blast at him, but it dissolved against the bars of the cage.

"Nice try." Andersen plunked down on a chair and unfolded a newspaper. "We're almost to the castle, so I think I'll just read the paper, if you don't mind. That way, if you try to plot your escape, I'll hear everything you say. Your teddy bear friend is dead, so don't think you're going to get saved by him."

Gasket growled at him, but Andersen just laughed.

I'm running out of time.

Andersen whistled as he turned a page.

As the train entered a tunnel, Theo saw a metal pipe running along the underside of the car. He climbed down and shimmied along it until he came up on the other side, between the car and the engine. Inside the engine car, a furnace glowed furiously. A pile of coal was stacked near it.

The train emerged from the tunnel and wound around a mountain. Stratus's castle loomed in the distance, and the moon hung over it, bigger than ever before.

Theo entered the engine car and turned the Whatsamadoozle into an ice scepter. He sprayed the furnace with a thin layer of ice, then climbed to the top of the passenger car and waited as the train started to slow down.

Andersen ran into the engine car. "What the blue bazooka—"

But the ice had melted by now, leaving no trace.

"Strange. I thought I put enough coal in."

As he shoveled in more coal, Theo dropped down and smacked the coupling several times as fast as he could.

Andersen whipped around at the sound of the hammering. "You're supposed to be dead!"

"So long," Theo said, whacking the coupling a final time. The cars disconnected.

"You can't rescue your friends without a key," Andersen said, waving a golden key in the air. He snickered.

Theo turned the Whatsamadoozle into a whip again and snatched the key out of Andersen's hand. "Thanks."

Enraged, Andersen howled while the engine barreled away. The passenger car slowed to a stop.

Heinrich and Bethany cheered as Theo unlocked the cage.

Gasket licked Theo gratefully, and Heinrich embraced him. "Oh, you're a miracle wrapped in fur!"

"I knew you'd rescue us, buddy. I didn't believe those clowns for one minute when they said you'd died."

"I'm sorry," Theo said. "I shouldn't have left you guys."

He looked at Lucinda, but she was facing the other way with her arms folded.

"What, you're not going to accept my apology?"

Lucinda puffed. "Apology! You could've gotten us killed!"

"And I apologized."

"You still don't get it," she said. "It's all about you. From the moment you came here, it's been all about you. You act like we exist only to serve you. Well, guess what? We have lives of our own, and you don't care about us. You only care about Grant—quit pretending. So no, I don't accept your apology."

A screeching sound outside could just be heard over Lucinda's rant. Heinrich looked out the back window and started to sweat. "Um—"

Lucinda ignored him. "And I'll tell you something else. We might as well have died. Our festival is ruined because of you!"

Theo bunched up his lips.

"That's right," Lucinda continued. "For the first time, you're speechless. It's nice to be able to talk for once."

Bethany joined Heinrich at the window. "Um, Lucinda—"

"Be quiet," she shouted. "I am tired of being nice. I'm going to speak my mind!"

Gasket joined Heinrich and Bethany at the window and whimpered.

"Go to the castle," Lucinda said, pointing to the window. "You're nearly there. And you'll probably get in, too. But leave us alone and let us live in peace."

Theo looked out the window. "You have to be kidding me."

The caboose was approaching, its turbo rockets blazing in the rear. Ludwig and Verona jumped on the roof, shouting frantically.

"You thought you could get rid of us," Ludwig said. "But we were prepared!"

"They're the most persistent clowns in the universe," Theo said, readying the Whatsamadoozle.

SMASH! The caboose crashed into the freight car, sending toy parts flying. CRASH! The freight car shot up the tracks, pushing the passenger car until it smashed into the engine car, where Andersen was standing with his arms folded. He coupled the car to the engine and entered. Ludwig and Verona coupled the caboose to the freight car, ran through it to the passenger car, and entered from the other side.

"What took you so long?" Andersen said, laughing. "You guys aren't going anywhere."

Andersen looked different now. He wore a robotic suit that

made him taller, his hands were claws, and his feet had become piston-actioned metal talons that screeched the ground as he walked. He put on a metal helmet with a glass cover that protected his face.

"Call me Robo Andersen."

"Yeah, Robo Andersen!" Verona echoed.

"I'd be scared right now if I were you," Ludwig said.

Andersen karate-chopped a booth in half and did a few roundhouse kicks for show. "I like it when my henchmen are agreeable. Hyuk hyuk."

Ludwig and Verona brandished knives, and Andersen assumed a karate pose.

Theo, Heinrich, Bethany, and Gasket stood with their backs together as the clowns approached them from both sides of the car.

"I'm still mad at you," Lucinda said to Theo.

"How about you be quiet and be mad at me later?" Theo said.

"I like that very much," Heinrich said, flexing his muscles.

"Save your squabbles," Bethany said, swinging her lasso. "We got bigger troubles right now."

Lucinda fired a dream blast at Andersen, but it dissolved against his suit.

"My turn to attack," Andersen said, running at her.

Theo readied the Whatsamadoozle, and then noticed the chandelier above. "Lucinda, shoot it!"

Lucinda fired a dream blast at the chandelier, but it didn't fall; instead, it just swung around.

"You really thought that would work?" Andersen said. He reached up, ripped the chandelier out of the ceiling, and threw it at them.

Theo turned the Whatsamadoozle into a claw, snatched the

chandelier out of the air, and hurled it against the wall. It shattered, and glass shards scattered across the carpet.

Andersen leaped at Lucinda, ready to kick her, but she held out her hands and fired a bigger dream blast at him, knocking him out of the air. She rolled under him as he crashed to his knees.

Theo turned the Whatsamadoozle into a mallet, and Lucinda fired a dream blast at it. It glowed purple, and Theo knew it was infused with magic.

Heinrich charged across the car and picked up Theo. He swung him around like a discus and threw him at Andersen. "One teddy bear with a side of Whatsamadoozle, coming right up!"

POW! Theo smashed into Andersen, and the clown staggered back. Then Heinrich headbutted him into the wall.

"Two ouchies for you," Heinrich said, uppercutting Andersen and following with a body slam. "Four ouchies, and many more to come until you give up your foolishness."

Theo turned the Whatsamadoozle into a sword and slashed Andersen across the chest.

"Watch the suit," the clown said, looking down at the slash. The suit was sparking.

WHAM! Ludwig crashed into Andersen and bounced off the suit. The clown lay groaning on the floor. "Sorry, boss . . ."

Bethany, perched on Gasket at the other end of the car, twirled her lasso and yelled, "Yee-haw! Serves you right, you stupid clown!"

Andersen's suit beeped, and it hummed as if it were charging. "Rats. I need more time." He dashed out of the car, and Lucinda and Heinrich flew after him.

"Where are you going?" Theo said, swinging the mallet. He was about to follow when he heard Gasket whimper; Verona was approaching Gasket with a knife, grinning. Bethany twirled her lasso again. Gasket looked as if he wanted to blow fire, but he couldn't because he would set the car ablaze.

Theo turned the Whatsamadoozle into a slingshot and pelted Verona on the back of the head.

"Ow!" Verona said, whipping around.

"Leave them alone," Theo said.

Verona bared her teeth and ran at Theo, but Gasket swiped her with his tail, knocking her down.

Bethany laughed and said, "Nice job beating the fat one, fellas."

Verona jumped to her feet and stomped, shaking the car. "No more jokes about my weight!"

"It ain't a joke," Bethany said, spinning her lasso. "It's the truth." She threw the lasso at Verona. Verona screamed, grabbed the lasso and yanked Bethany off Gasket and into a booth, breaking it.

"Ouch . . ."

Bethany tried to stagger up as Verona marched toward her.

Theo turned the Whatsamadoozle into the giant kissing cockroach. The roach made a smooching sound as it tapped her on the shoulder.

"I'm busy right now," Verona said, not turning around.

The cockroach tapped her on the shoulder again and she whipped around. Seeing the bug, all the color in her face drained and she dropped her knife.

POW! Bethany punched her then grabbed the clown by the feet and dragged her outside the car, puffing as she heaved Verona across the floor.

"Let me go!"

"This is payback for kidnapping Gasket," Bethany said, pulling harder.

Verona kicked Bethany, almost knocking her off the train.

Bethany stumbled back and Verona jumped on top of her, pulling her hair.

Theo turned the Whatsamadoozle into a Taser and zapped Verona. She twitched involuntarily as Bethany rolled from underneath her.

"Good riddance," Bethany said, kicking her over.

"You're going to pay for that!" cried a voice. Ludwig had sneaked up behind Theo. He jumped into the air, ready to stab him.

CRACK!

The lasso whizzed over Theo's head. Bethany roped Ludwig out of midair and whipped him off the train.

"Adios," she said. She gave Theo a high five. "We sure gave those misfits a roundup, didn't we?"

Gasket licked her.

Their celebration was interrupted by clashing on the roof. Theo turned the Whatsamadoozle into a propeller and flew outside, where Beasley and Heinrich were boxing. Andersen and Lucinda were cheering them on.

POW! POW! Heinrich and Beasley took turns wailing on each other.

Andersen snickered and a pistol popped out of his suit. He aimed it at Heinrich.

Theo turned the Whatsamadoozle into a hundred-pound weight and landed on Andersen, crushing him.

"Ow . . ."

Heinrich uppercut Beasley, and the clown staggered backward. Lucinda hit Beasley with a dream blast, knocking him off the train.

Andersen's suit glowed. An electric blast zapped Theo away.

"I'm fully charged now," Andersen said. "It's time to end this."

The suit beeped, and an electric force field appeared around Andersen. He assumed another karate pose and kicked the air a few times. Then he spun and kicked Heinrich, who shook as volts surged through his body.

Theo swung the Whatsamadoozle at Andersen, but the clown jumped back and assaulted Theo with quick karate chops and kicks. Theo ducked, rolled, and jumped out of the way as the clown hi-yahed maniacally.

"I'm invincible now," Andersen said. He looked at Theo. "My offer still stands. You can join me now, and I'll promise your friends a quick death."

Theo turned the Whatsamadoozle into a high-pressure water hose. "Never."

WHOOSH! Theo sprayed water on Andersen, and the force field sparked violently before disappearing. The suit beeped and lost all its power. Andersen leaped out. "My suit! You drained the power from it. Now it has to charge all over again." He grunted and pulled out a pistol, aiming it at Theo. "This one's loaded. Hyuk hyuk."

He'd just put his finger on the trigger when Gasket swooped down and engulfed him in fire. The clown screamed and dropped the pistol off the side of the train.

Gasket landed, and Bethany slapped the roof of the train with her rope. "That's for kidnapping Gasket, you stupid clown!" Bethany shouted.

The toys approached Andersen and he stumbled backward. "I'll never give you the satisfaction," he said.

The train crossed a bridge; a rushing river ran far below. Andersen leaped off the train. A parachute popped out of his clown suit, and he waved as the wind carried him away.

Bethany spat in Andersen's direction. "And don't come back!" she shouted.

Theo patted Gasket. "Good work, pal."

"We gave them the ouchies of a lifetime," Heinrich said.

Theo sheathed the Whatsamadoozle. He saw Andersen's metal suit, still propped on its knees at the edge of the car.

Theo pushed the suit over the side of the car, and it whistled as it plummeted into the river below. The current took it and eddied it downstream into a drain under the castle.

Lucinda glanced ahead. "We're almost there."

"This is your chance, Theo," Bethany said. "You'll be able to rescue Grant now."

This really is my chance.

In just a few minutes, the train would enter the courtyard of the castle and he'd be inside. All he would have to do was find Grant and they'd be able to escape this place once and for all.

The Whatsamadoozle glowed in his hand, and he sighed deeply at the thought that it would almost be over—the final battle.

But then he thought of the caravan.

No. I owe them. I need to make sure they are safe first.

He deactivated the Whatsamadoozle and looked the other way.

"What are you doin'?" Bethany asked. "This is your chance!"

Theo jumped on Gasket. "What are you guys waiting on? We've got a festival to run."

10

A DISCOVERY

Jiskyl worked among the festival ruins, trying to rebuild the big top by himself, but it kept falling over on him.

"You're back," he said sardonically when he saw everyone. "You might as well have stayed on the train."

Heinrich picked up his mallet from a pile of stones and shook his head. Bethany kicked one of the stones and cursed.

Lucinda hovered over to the big tent. Seeing the extent of the damage, she began to cry. "It was all for nothing."

Her sobs hurt Theo; he dug his foot into the gravel and looked away.

Jiskyl put a hand on Lucinda's shoulder. "There, there. I was too negative, my dear. Perhaps we can still salvage things."

"No. It's ruined." She whipped around and pointed at Theo. "It's your fault!"

Theo tried not to look at her, but she was on top of him in an instant, hitting his chest.

"It's all because of your selfishness!"

"Get off me!"

Heinrich pulled her away, but she kept swinging.

"Not once did you ever ask why we were even putting on this festival!"

Theo rubbed his chest. "I guess now's a better time than any." He rolled his eyes and said, "Please, Lucinda. Tell me all about this festival and why it's so important to you."

Lucinda fired a dream blast and knocked him into a midway stand. "Gee, I'll tell you, Mr. Know-It-All. The festival is to honor one of our dead friends."

"I know that already. How did he die?"

"He sacrificed himself to save us," Lucinda said.

"You mentioned that in the lodge," Theo said, rubbing his head. "Are you going to tell me what happened, or are you going to keep being cryptic?"

Jiskyl leaned on his cane and said, "It's a long story. Several years ago, we were in this very spot, eating our supper, when a little boy staggered up to us. Just by looking at him, it was clear that he had escaped the castle. Heaven knows how he did it. He kept screaming . . . I can still hear his screams even now."

"We took him in," Lucinda said. "And the only person who could calm him was our friend—Mazeltop. He was the oldest of us, and his fatherly tone calmed the boy. We fed the kid and did tricks for him, and he opened up to us. He told us about the terrible things that Stratus had done to him. You couldn't imagine the nightmares he had seen. We knew he'd never be the same as long as Stratus kept a grip on his mind. He told us that he missed his family. And he mentioned a portal in the castle—the only way to escape. We knew what it felt like to miss a loved one, so we decided to help him, even though it meant risking our lives. We snuck him into the castle, and when we made it to the portal in the throne room, Stratus appeared. He would have suffocated us all if Mazeltop hadn't jumped in the way."

Jiskyl sighed. "The last thing he said was, 'Never lose hope.'"

"The sight of Stratus sent the boy out of his mind," Lucinda said. "He started screaming again, so we pushed him through the portal. He escaped. But we weren't so lucky."

Jiskyl pointed to the scars on his face. "Stratus tortured us for days and then released us as an example for other toys who dared to cross him."

Heinrich spat. "The other toys in the Stratusphere shunned us, and we were forced to wander this place forever."

"I can't believe he tortured you guys like that."

Lucinda turned the other way. "We can bear our punishment. But the real sufferer was the kid—all the kids that Stratus kidnapped, really. Stratus puts evil thoughts in their minds, and even if they were to escape, they'd probably never be the same." She looked at Theo intensely. "That's why we have the festival. This is a crappy existence, Theo. But despite that, we never lose hope, even though we hate this place. Even though we're scared every day of what can happen, even though Stratus's goons get stronger every day, we never back down. And this is the only night of the year where we can forget our fears and celebrate the memory of Mazeltop—and that boy, the only human to ever escape the Stratusphere."

Theo squinted. "Surely he couldn't have been the only one."

"That's why Stratus tortured us," Lucinda said. "Because we helped Shawn escape."

"Shawn!"

"Why do you have repeat and scream everything I say?"

"I don't believe you."

"Why not? Here we go again—it's all about you, isn't it?"

"Shawn was my first owner," Theo said. "He was abducted . . . by Stratus."

Everyone gasped. Heinrich put his hands on his head and said, "Oh mein gott!"

"I couldn't rescue him. I've never forgiven myself."

"Some Ursabrand you are," Lucinda said, puffing. "Does that sound familiar?"

"He was never the same when he returned. He hated me. Now he's a teenager and he never plays with his toys. Stratus changed him."

"That is the natural progression of all children," Jiskyl said. "Stratus just accelerates it."

Theo stared at the moon. "Shawn gave me to Grant because he hated me so much. I swore that I would never let anything happen to Grant, and yet I'm here."

"Why didn't you follow Stratus through when he stole Shawn?" Bethany asked.

Theo's voice broke but he kept it together. "I was . . . I was sleeping. I didn't know until the portal had closed, until after it was too late."

Bethany slapped Theo on the back. "Don't beat yourself up. That happened to me, too. Happened to us all in some way or another. That's how Stratus is. Finds toys who can't defend their owners, and then he takes advantage."

Theo rubbed his head. He felt so moved by everything that he didn't know what else to say. "Lucinda, you were right to be angry with me. You saved Shawn. I am grateful to you."

"You don't have to hide everything," she said. "You're not the first toy to come here with a shattered past. You're not alone."

Theo swallowed. He couldn't find words to speak.

Lucinda sighed softly and glanced again at the festival grounds. "I don't know how we'll finish the festival now. Everyone will be here soon."

Theo turned the Whatsamadoozle into a mallet and hammered in a stake.

"There's no use," Lucinda said.

Theo shook his head. "Remember what Mazeltop said? Don't lose hope. We've got a lot of work to do, but we've got to do it—for Mazeltop, for Shawn, and for all of toykind."

11

FESTIVAL OF SHADOWS

They worked without stopping until everything was up and running again. The carousel stuttered, but it ran; the midway lit up even though it was still in ruins.

Heinrich swept the grounds as fast as he could. Bethany set up a sawhorse and sawed wood, then tossed it to Lucinda, who painted it and quick-dried the paint with her magic. Theo threw the wood into a wheelbarrow and ran down the midway, where he and Jiskyl rebuilt the stands.

Soon, everything was functional, though it looked kind of sad.

"It's the best we can do," Lucinda said.

Visitors streamed in from the dark plains. They were all toys with interesting and unique injuries, and they looked around and smiled. Even though the festival wasn't perfect, no one turned away.

The caravan toys stood in front of their attractions, calling out to passersby.

"We had a few setbacks, but you'll still have fun!"

"Come and watch me ring the bell!"

"Want to fly on a dragon? Get out your coins!"

More toys came, and soon the place bustled with noise and laughter.

Theo sat in the back of a wagon and watched from the outskirts. Despite all the damage, despite the festival's ragged appearance, the visiting toys were having fun. They rode the carousel and played the games in the midway, and they happily paid coins for everything.

He didn't know why, but it was sad. All these toys were trying to create a semblance of their former lives in this bleak dimension where the truth was obvious. When it was all over, when the lights were turned off, when the caravan moved on to its next location, these toys would go back to living in fear, back to the reality of the Stratusphere. And beyond, in the dark places of this world where there was no goodness, other toys were probably celebrating evil things—all because they chose the side that offered them safety, even if that safety came at a terrible price.

He prayed that he would never end up like the caravan toys. He didn't like the idea of having to make such a choice about his fate.

In the distance, Lucinda stood on a platform and spoke into a megaphone.

"I want to take a moment to remember our dear friend who couldn't be with us tonight. Everything you see is in his honor. Through his memory, we are reminded to never lose hope, to always smile, to always make the best of our situation—no matter how discarded or abandoned we feel. Though we may be surrounded by eternal darkness, we must always represent the light. Let's cheer for Mazeltop and the rest of our friends who have died!"

"Yippee!"

Lucinda hovered upward. "One more cheer for hope!"

"Woo hoo!"

Lucinda flew higher and fired several dream blasts into the sky; they exploded into fireworks, and everyone oohed and aahed.

The toys grabbed her, cheering. She blushed and laughed as she lost herself in the huge crowd.

It was the perfect time to leave. Theo jumped off the wagon and looked up at the moon.

It was nice to know all of you.

He turned to leave when he heard a voice. "Leaving, eh?"

It was Jiskyl.

"I fulfilled my duties," Theo said.

"Yes, and now it's time for me to fulfill mine."

Jiskyl handed him a golden, decorated shield with a dragon on the front. "It once belonged to a knight. You'll need it."

Theo held the shield; along with the Whatsamadoozle, it felt right.

"You can enter the castle through the Dream Marshes."

"I tried that, but Shaggy ambushed me there."

"You were on the north end of the marshes," Jiskyl said. "You need to go to the south end. You can access the castle through a sewer drain. On my way here, I passed by it and I assure you that it's still unguarded. You can get to the lower level of the castle from the sewers. Just be careful when you get inside—heaven knows what lurks in those filthy canals."

"Thanks, Jiskyl."

The old fish nodded and shook Theo's hand. "You might save us all, or you might be headed to your grave—I still can't figure you out. But in any case, it was nice to meet you."

Theo looked back at the festival, where everyone was having fun and laughing and playing. The sound of music and the smell of cotton candy blended into the night, and part of him wished he could have stayed, enjoyed the company of friends. But he knew what he had to do.

Theo saluted Jiskyl, and then started down the path to the Dream Marshes, thinking of Grant.

12

SLUICING AROUND

Theo made his way through the Dream Marshes, and just outside the castle he found the drain that Jiskyl had told him about. He turned the Whatsamadoozle into a saw and cut himself an entrance.

The drain was dark and wide. He turned the Whatsamadoozle into a flashlight and climbed in. After a while, he emerged in a sewer system. Marsh water gushed in thick streams, and green-stoned walkways flanked the channels on either side. The streams crisscrossed each other at perpendicular angles, and here and there were capstans—some working, some broken—that looked as if they controlled the water somehow. On the far side of the system, Theo saw an iron door with moons all over it—it had to lead upstairs to the castle.

I've got to get to that door.

He would have to get past the streams, but he knew that if he touched the marsh water it would send him into hallucinations. He prepared to jump, but then he stopped. The distance was too far.

He turned the Whatsamadoozle into a propeller and was

ready to take off when a school of shimmering piranhas splashed out of the water, chomping. They eyed Theo, waiting for him.

They'll eat me alive if I try to cross.

He ran down a pathway. It dead-ended at a capstan, but its wooden handles were missing.

This probably controls the water flow, but it's broken. How am I supposed to get across?

He heard a jangling sound behind him and ducked into an alcove as a blue blob with an eye patch rounded a corner. Its mouth was a dripping mess, and its breath—a mixture of raw sewage, rotten food, and burning plastic—made Theo gag. It carried a lantern in one hand and a wooden bucket filled with tools in the other. The blob grumbled as it walked, leaving a trail of steaming slime after it. As it got closer to Theo, he could read the name written sloppily on both the lantern and the bucket: Fogerty.

"Here it is," Fogerty said, stopping at the lever. He set the bucket down, reached into his throat, and pulled out a slimy clipboard. "Sluice gate ten thousand, five hundred and sixty-six. This one ain't so bad. All it needs is an Allen wrench."

He dug through the bucket of tools and pulled out a huge Allen wrench. He slid it into the capstan and strained to push it clockwise until it rotated twice. Below, the marsh water stopped flowing, revealing a walkway with a door set into one of the walls.

Fogerty gazed toward another capstan in the distance. "Better keep going if I want to eat some toys for lunch."

He sludged his way toward the next capstan.

Theo dropped down where the water had been. The piranhas were gone. He tugged on the metal door, pulling several times before it clanged open. Beyond it lay a small room with a yellow ladder. Theo climbed the ladder into the ceiling and came to another iron door. He opened it and stepped into a small alcove, ducking as Fogerty passed.

The next capstan was nearby—he had taken a shortcut.

Fogerty set down his bucket and inspected the broken lever. "I think this one needs a good hammering." He pulled out a hammer and banged several of the capstan's bars until it moved.

Below, the marsh water stopped flowing. Fogerty turned the capstan and a small bridge extended from the ground, connecting the two walkways. The walkway led to another broken capstan. Once it was opened Theo would be able to make it to the door.

"That's the one that needs the sprocket," Fogerty said, sludging across the bridge.

This is the last one. I need to take him out.

POW! Theo turned the Whatsamadoozle into a mallet and smacked Fogerty in the back, knocking him off the bridge. He caught Fogerty's bucket in midair.

"Thanks."

Fogerty splattered onto the ground below and tried to form himself back together. "You rotten plush-bucket . . ."

Theo crossed the bridge and turned the Whatsamadoozle into a whip, lashed it across the way, and grabbed the capstan, turning it several times. Marsh water flowed below, washing Fogerty away. He screamed as he disappeared down a tunnel.

Theo ran to the final capstan. The top was exposed, revealing a gear box with an empty circular space where an object should have been.

He looked in the bucket. "He said it needed a sprocket. Okay, here's one. But what goes with a sprocket?"

He used an Allen wrench, but the capstan wouldn't budge. He cycled through all the tools, finally finding the correct one—a chain—but it took a long time.

A bridge extended and he ran across to the door. It was

massive, with an image of the night sky etched into the metal. There was a slot for a circular object in the middle of the door.

Theo remembered the coin purse that Jiskyl had given him; he unloaded the coins into his palm and scanned them, inspecting each coin until he found the right one—a coin with a star embossed on it.

The coin lit up inside the slot, and the door creaked open.

Behind him, the water turned to sludge. Fogerty's face appeared in the current, and the blob rose high into the air, towering over Theo. He was huge now, a wall of sludge and slime. He put on his eye patch and roared.

"How dare you sneak into the castle?"

Theo readied the Whatsamadoozle.

A big, slimy arm extended from Fogerty's body. He ripped a capstan out of the floor and hurled it, wedging it inside the doorway and blocking Theo from passing. Fogerty raised his arm again, but Theo rolled out of the way, slashing his sword at the arm. The sword went through it, but it didn't affect Fogerty.

"Your physical attacks will not work on me, plush-bucket."

Theo turned the Whatsamadoozle into a magic scepter and tried to think of a spell.

He's blue, and he's probably aligned with water. What type of spell would work on him?

Theo waved the scepter and thought of the earth. The ground shook. Stalagmites jutted out of the floor and pierced Fogerty, sending slime everywhere.

It worked.

But not for long. Suddenly, all the slime gathered back into a blob and Fogerty's face reappeared, laughing.

"Is that the best you can do?"

Let's try this again.

Theo waved the scepter and thought of wind. A tornado blew through the tunnel, slicing Fogerty into tiny blobs. When the wind faded, the blobs reassembled and Fogerty's face appeared again. He rose over Theo, laughing.

"You're pathetic, plush-bucket." Fogerty prepared to crush Theo.

One more time!

Theo waved the scepter and thought of electricity. Lightning struck Fogerty several times, and the blob screamed in pain. Each zap sent loads of slime flying everywhere, smoking and splattering against the walls, the floor, and the ceiling.

"Finally," Theo said.

But Fogerty regathered again and laughed. "That hurt—I'll admit it. But that's not enough to defeat me, bear."

I need to try something different.

The stream near Theo flowed with assorted garbage and junk. Among the trash was a familiar silver object—Andersen's metal suit. It was floating on the surface, and Theo wondered if it still worked.

How did it end up here?

Fogerty swiped at Theo, but Theo dodged, turned the Whatsamadoozle into a giant claw, and snatched the suit out of the water. He jumped into the suit and it activated around him. The arms and legs sprang to life, one at a time. The glass visor shut over his face, and through the glass, Theo saw the capstans, with yellow targets positioned over them.

Then he got a whiff of the suit's interior—a mixture of sweat, makeup, and smelly feet. He almost gagged. He'd have to hold his breath.

Theo turned the Whatsamadoozle into a sword and stood in front of Fogerty, slashing the air.

"Interesting contraption," Fogerty said. "But it won't work on me." He smacked a nearby capstan, then flowed into a tunnel and emerged on the other side, this time glowing red.

"How did you change colors?" Theo asked. His voice was metallic now that it was filtered through the suit.

Fogerty spewed fire at Theo, but it didn't damage the suit. A blinking progress bar appeared across his field of vision. On the end of the progress bar was a picture of the suit with electricity all around it.

It's charging. Twenty-five percent.

Fogerty punched the suit, knocking Theo back. Theo spun a roundhouse kick and cut Fogerty's arm in half, then jumped into the air and slammed a metal fist into Fogerty's jaw. The blob laughed, snatched him out of the air, and threw him against the wall.

Fifty percent.

Fogerty smacked another capstan and turned brown. A stalagmite javelin appeared in his hand, and he threw it.

Seventy-five percent.

Theo caught the javelin in midair. He scanned the capstans in the area; a symbol appeared over each one.

Which one will turn Fogerty blue again?

He kicked a capstan with a triangle over it, and Fogerty turned green and breathed heavy gusts that made Theo stagger back.

"Stop resisting!" Fogerty cried.

Theo dashed away and kicked another capstan with a circle over it.

Fogerty turned red again and spewed fire that burned the suit, but didn't cause damage.

"Nice try!"

This is getting old.

He kicked another capstan with wavy lines over it, and Fogerty finally changed to blue.

Perfect.

The suit beeped, and an electric force field appeared around it. Theo charged into Fogerty and sent a high-voltage current through the blob, frying him. The voltage shot tiny blobs everywhere, and Fogerty roared and shrank until only his eyes and mouth remained.

"Leave me alone," Theo said, standing over the blob.

"You may have defeated me, but you will still die, plushbucket."

Fogerty's mouth and eyes slid into a nearby stream, and the current carried him away. "I hate teddy bears . . ."

"That was easy," Theo said. He ran to the door and used the suit to karate-chop the capstan that blocked the doorway. Then he jumped out of the suit and ran upstairs.

13

AN UNEXPECTED FOE

Inside the castle, Theo opened a wooden door and climbed a spiral staircase; it led into a long, torch-lit hallway with purple carpet. There were no windows, so the air was stuffy. There was no one around.

He turned the Whatsamadoozle into a sword and crept down the hallway toward an iron door. He heard distant screams that wrenched his gut. They were children.

The door was ajar; Theo peeked inside. Dozens of children, all tied to the wall with their eyes closed, screamed constantly, as if nightmares were playing on their eyelids.

So this is what Stratus does to them.

The children's screams were deafening. Using the sword, he cut them from the wall. They began to snore as they hit the ground.

I wonder what they were seeing.

But he didn't pursue the thought, understanding that he'd be better off if he never knew. Another iron door at the end of the room opened. Theo readied his sword and ran through it, into the throne room. Grant lay sleeping on the floor.

"Grant!"

He rushed to Grant's side. "I'm going to get you out of here, buddy."

He pushed Grant's shoulders, but nothing happened. The boy wouldn't wake up.

He must still be under a spell.

Theo heard a noise and turned just in time to see a torch flying at him. He held up his shield and the torch bounced off.

"I cannot believe you made it this far," said a familiar voice. "Very impressive."

Theo squinted into the shadows. "That voice . . ."

Topperson, Grant's top, spun out of the shadows. "Hello, Theo."

Grant's body shimmered with white light, and he disappeared.

"Topperson!"

"You didn't listen to me when I told you that this place was dangerous. Now you can see why I gave you that advice."

"But I don't understand—"

"You are foolish, that's why. An entire charade played before your eyes, and you still don't understand."

Theo fell silent and listened.

"Stratus planted me in your house so that I could procure Grant when the time was right."

"But why did you give in to the dark side?"

"I betrayed Stratus once, and I learned my lesson. He showed me my foolishness. Here, in the Stratusphere, we toys live forever. We want for nothing. And the only person we must ever please is Stratus, who will never grow old or abandon us. It's a grand way of life when you ignore the many evils of this place, Theo."

He betrayed Stratus?

"I orchestrated your little adventure in the basement," Topperson said. "When Shawn was here many years ago,

Stratus planted subconscious instructions for him: during Grant's ninth year, Shawn was to throw you into the basement on the shortest night of the year. That way, there would be no chance of rescue."

"And when I was down there, you summoned Stratus."

"Indeed. Not even His Grace planned for you to make it here before sunrise. Optimistic toys like you are such an impediment." Topperson spun around the room as he talked. "Don't misunderstand me, Theo. I'm not evil. All I've ever wanted for Grant was the best. I want him to grow up, forget all about us, and live a successful, toyless life."

"So why did you do it?"

"Look at me. I'm old. I deserve to spend my final days in a place where I am valued. You do, too."

"So you would betray your owner to do it? Grant loves you."

"Until the day he doesn't. One day, he would have woken up and abandoned us. All children do. You and I would have been hauled off to the junkyard—or worse, a daycare. When will you learn that Stratus can offer us a life in this world that no child can? Give up your petty factory settings and listen to me, Theo. You're fighting for a hopeless cause. Shawn has already moved on and forgotten us—Stratus's efforts with him were successful." Fire lit behind his gears, giving him a sinister glow.

"Wait," Theo said. "You didn't come to the house until after Shawn was kidnapped . . . You couldn't have known about him, unless—" His eyes widened. "You're not Topperson."

The top laughed. "Finally, you are beginning to understand this strange world around you. No, I am not Topperson. My name is Mazeltop."

"No," Theo said, taken aback. "You were good. Jiskyl said so many nice things about you. He risked his life so that we could have a festival in your honor. A hundred toys just gathered and celebrated in your name!"

"And I am touched," Mazeltop said. "But they should have been praising His Grace."

"There is still time to undo what you've done," Theo said. "Surrender Grant to me."

Mazeltop spun faster. "I can't do that."

"Then it pains me to end it this way," Theo said, unsheathing his sword.

Mazeltop struck the wall. A torch fell down on the carpet and flames bloomed in a circle around them, preventing either of them from escaping.

Mazeltop dashed toward Theo; Theo slashed, and Mazeltop recoiled.

Theo slashed again, but Mazeltop spun away quickly, digging into the floor. Sparks shot at Theo, shocking the Whatsamadoozle out of his hand.

Mazeltop dashed at him again but Theo hid behind his shield, knocking Mazeltop back. Theo swiped the Whatsamadoozle off the ground and turned it into a pogo stick. He hopped into the air, turned the Whatsamadoozle into a hundred-pound weight, and landed on Mazeltop, sending plastic parts everywhere.

Mazeltop tried to keep spinning, but he couldn't. Theo turned the Whatsamadoozle into a fire extinguisher, put out the flames, and stood over the fallen top.

"Finish me," Mazeltop said, gasping. "I am broken beyond repair now."

Theo nodded and turned the Whatsamadoozle into a sword. He raised it to stab, but shadows engulfed the room and something struck him in the back, knocking him out.

14

SHATTER THE DARKNESS

Theo lay unconscious on the ground. The room filled with shadows and fog, and Stratus appeared, grinning. He floated over Theo and streamed dark energy into his head. Theo tossed and turned in the grip of night terrors.

Mazeltop cheered Stratus on. "Finish him, My Lord!"

Stratus filled the room with his booming laughter. He reached for Theo's neck, but a blue blast struck his hands.

"Leave him alone."

Stratus whipped around and shook with rage when he saw Lucinda, Heinrich, Bethany, Gasket, and Jiskyl standing in the throne room.

Jiskyl stepped forward. "Mazeltop . . ."

Mazeltop sparked. "Old friend, you mustn't blame me for my actions. Everything I did, I did for all toykind."

"I risked my life to honor your memory. You betrayed me. You betrayed everyone. You got what you deserve."

Mazeltop glanced up at Stratus. "Your Grace, please honor me for my sacrifice."

Stratus dissipated and then gathered behind Mazeltop, dark energy surging into his hands.

"Yes, Your Grace! Embrace me with your power. Make me live forever . . . What are you—no, Your Grace! Please! Aaaah . . ."

Stratus covered Mazeltop with shadows. There was a crushing sound, then Stratus tossed Mazeltop's crumpled remains at Lucinda's feet, and the top was no more.

Shadows spiraled under Stratus as he floated toward the toys. He pointed at them in a command to bow.

"We've lived in fear of you for too long," Lucinda said. "No more."

Stratus gave them an evil glare. He demanded them to bow again, but they readied themselves. His hands turned into shadowy scythes and his eyes flashed red.

On the floor, Theo twitched and cried out.

"Wake up, Theo," Lucinda whispered, worried. "Please. I don't know how long we'll be able to hold him off."

Theo opened his eyes. He was flying headfirst through darkness. He heard his voice in the depths, reflecting back at him.

I'm useless. I can't protect anyone.

His eyes widened at the sound of his voice and the words that he hadn't said. "But I tried."

His own voice responded. It was cold, defeated. *Trying wasn't good enough.*

"I was so close. Stratus was within my reach."

And for the second time, I lost.

"But it wasn't like the last time—I was stronger."

He picked up speed.

Strength doesn't matter. I still lost.

"But I have so much more to live for."

Like what?

"I can't let Grant down. I can't give up on my new friends."

An Ursabrand cannot focus on friends.

"No—you're wrong."

I'm violating the oath. I've lost sight of my goals so much. I deserve to die.

He stopped floating. The darkness peeled away into a screen that showed Shawn's bedroom. It was nighttime, and Theo saw himself sleeping in young Shawn's arms.

They looked so happy. Shawn snored, and Theo nestled into Shawn's shoulder, a smile on his face even in sleep. A portal opened under the bed and Stratus snatched Shawn in an instant, and Theo slid down onto the bed. Instead of waking up, he snuggled with the pillow.

Look at me. I didn't even know what was happening. Everything was perfect then.

"I don't want to watch this."

But the screen kept playing, and Theo kept watching himself sleeping, kept watching that happy curve of a smile on his face. The longer it was on the screen, the worse he felt.

Then the screen melted and the darkness returned. Self-doubt stung him as he journeyed farther into the darkness.

* * *

Stratus moved with supernatural speed, and the toys narrowly dodged his slices. He was nowhere and everywhere at once. It was impossible to hit him.

Heinrich tried to headbutt Stratus's arm, but Stratus smacked him against the wall.

Lucinda fired a dream blast; Stratus lashed at her, but Bethany pulled her out of the way just in time.

"I don't know how much longer we're going to be able to fight," Bethany said. "He's darn near invincible."

Stratus laughed at Bethany's compliment and lunged for

her. Gasket blew fire at him, but Stratus dissipated and swung at Jiskyl instead, who waved his cane and shot lightning bolts at him.

Theo convulsed on the floor, and Lucinda glanced back at him. "I believe in you."

Stratus laughed and flowed toward her as she fired another dream blast, engulfing the room in blue light.

* * *

Theo touched down on Shawn's bed. Time sped up, and Theo saw Shawn zip out of the portal under the bed. He moved in and out of the room as the years passed. He blinked, flickered out of sight, and then appeared on the bed sitting next to Theo. The sun slid into the sky, and dawn light washed over the room.

Shawn looked at Theo and played with his hands, as if he didn't know what to say.

"What happened between us, old pal?" Theo asked.

"I grew up."

"I guess it happened faster than I thought it would."

"Yeah."

Silence grew between them, and it was some time before Theo spoke. "I want you to know that I'm sorry that I couldn't protect you."

Shawn sighed. "I went through hell because of you. You can't even imagine the nightmares I saw. They changed me. But maybe it was meant to happen."

Theo hopped down from the bed and climbed up on the windowsill. He gazed at the cars passing by. "Maybe some things do happen for a reason. The longer I'm in the Stratusphere, the more I realize that." He gestured around the room. "I tried to hold on to all of this. I wanted it to last forever. Same with Grant. But the more I try to hold on, the more everything turns to smoke that slips between my fingers."

"You and me both."

"Yeah."

Shawn brightened a little. "Don't blame yourself. All of this, it wasn't going to last anyway. You were better off with Grant."

"Yeah, I was. You never liked teddy bears, anyway."

Shawn laughed. The room dissolved, and Theo watched himself on a screen again. Grant was holding him, and he brought him up to his face, smiling. There was none of Shawn's heaviness; Grant was pure kid, full of happiness and laughter.

I remember this. This was after Shawn gave me to Grant.

"I made you something," Grant said. He handed Theo a wooden sword and shield. "Since you're an Ursabrand, your duty is to protect me and the toys from the boogie man. With these, you can protect us all."

Theo remained stiff, but he wanted to smile.

"Now repeat after me," Grant said. "I, Theodorus Ursabrand, promise to protect Grant and the toys, no matter what happens, even if it means sacrificing my life!"

Theo was silent.

"There," Grant said. "Now you're under oath."

He made Theo slash his sword and bring his shield up. "And don't forget to practice. You'll need your skills. And when things get rough, just think of home, and me, your best buddy!"

Mom called from the kitchen. "Dinner time!"

"Be back, buddy."

Grant shut the door and Theo gripped the sword and shield, feeling them for the first time again. It was odd, revisiting this memory.

He jumped down to the floor. He tried to slash the sword, but it was so heavy he fell down. He struggled to get up; the shield was heavy, too.

He slashed again and lost his balance. For two hours, he practiced fighting with the sword until it was comfortable in his hands and its weight was no longer a burden. All the while, he kept repeating the oath.

Then everything faded to darkness. He flew headfirst again, and his voice resounded from beyond.

Now I remember the oath. Now I remember why I am doing all of this. Because I was a failure.

"I don't need to keep hearing that."

I'm not fighting because I love Grant. I'm fighting to mask my own failure to protect Shawn.

"I said I didn't want to hear it!"

Theo punched the air, but his voice continued.

I should offer my services to Stratus. I can save Grant this way.

"No."

Then I should offer him my head. I can die with a shred of dignity. I said I'd never want to make this choice, but here I am. The darkness is so inviting. What am I waiting for? Turn or die!

Theo slanted his eyes. "That's not me talking. I refuse to believe that! Who are you?"

The darkness in front of Theo condensed into a red eye, and he heard Stratus's laughter.

"No. This is an illusion. Why didn't I realize it sooner?"

Stratus's laughter grew louder. Theo felt the Whatsamadoozle glowing in his hand—it had been at his side all along. "I know why I'm fighting. I'm not just fighting for Grant. I'm not even fighting for myself anymore." He stared at Stratus's eye. "I'm fighting for everyone you've hurt. I won't let you win."

He heard Lucinda's voice and the sound of fighting. The darkness shattered around him, and he was lying on his back in the throne room. The toys huddled in a corner, out of breath and zapped of their energy. Stratus rose over them and turned his hand into a hammer. He raised it and brought it down toward them. The toys closed their eyes.

Theo clutched his golden shield, and in an instant, he was in front of the toys with the shield in front of his face.

Stratus struck the shield. It glowed, flooding the area with light, and the impact knocked him backward.

The shield blinked rapidly and a golden sword pulsed in Theo's hand.

"Thanks for believing in me," Theo said to Lucinda.

Lucinda staggered up and stood next to him. The other toys did the same, even though they could barely walk.

"Welcome back, sleepyhead," Jiskyl said.

Stratus pounded the floor and the castle shook; the walls disconnected, the floor dissolved, and the ceiling crumbled into an ethereal skyscape full of nebulae. The ground turned into craggy rock, leaving the toys standing on a cliff that overlooked nothingness.

Stratus rose higher and higher. He transformed into a shadow dragon with glowing red eyes, smoky breath, and a ferocious roar. He hovered over the cliff, breathing shadow fire.

The toys readied themselves again, and Theo pointed his sword at Stratus.

"It ends now."

"How the heck are we gonna defeat him?" Bethany said, slapping her lasso.

"Never lose hope," Theo said. "Remember?"

Bethany nodded and climbed onto Gasket, who flapped his wings and blew fire angrily.

Heinrich ran to Theo's side. "I am lucky to have met a friend like you. Up you go, my little cub!" He picked Theo up and launched him toward the dragon's mouth, shouting, "When this is over, I want my Whatsamadoozle back!"

Theo slashed the dragon. It roared with pain, but grew

taller. Theo couldn't reach the dragon's head anymore, and he fell backward toward the nothingness.

He landed on Gasket, who flew upward as Bethany yee-hawed.

"No matter what happens," Bethany said, "we'll have your back. Let's make this place a world worth living in."

Gasket blew fire at the dragon's torso. It roared and tried to swipe them out of the sky, but Bethany flung her lasso and wrapped it around one of the beast's claws. She yanked with all her might and pulled it toward Gasket.

"You have to keep going. I won't be able to hold him for long."

Theo leaped onto the dragon's arm and ran up. The dragon blew fire at him and he hid behind his shield, waiting for the burning to begin.

But the fire never touched Theo. There was a blue flash, and the fire turned to a giant ice crystal that hung suspended in the air, spiraling up to the dragon's mouth.

Jiskyl waved at Theo from below. "Are you still sleepwalking?" the old fish said. "Keep climbing!"

Theo climbed the ice quickly, avoiding the dragon's claws as they broke the ice behind him. When he was level with the dragon's head he jumped into the air, ready to drive his sword deep into its skull, but the dragon grabbed him with its claws and squeezed him.

A dream blast struck the dragon's claws. The dragon let go of Theo, and he began to fall again.

Another dream blast hit Theo in the back, knocking him upward. Then another. And another. The barrage of dream blasts brought him high over the dragon's head again, and he shot downward toward its crown.

"One more blow," Lucinda said from below. She fired a dream blast into Theo's sword, and it glowed blue.

Theo drove the sword into the top of the dragon's head. It screamed as shadows flowed out of its body. Theo dug the sword in hard and deep, and the dragon jerked, throwing him off.

Theo landed on Gasket, who had circled up to meet him, and they flew down to the other toys. They all watched as the dragon dissolved before their eyes. Its roar, once deafening, diminished to a whisper, and the skyscape, once vivid and colorful, faded slowly to black.

A portal back to the throne room appeared behind them.

"It's over," Theo said, sheathing his sword.

"We've got to get out of here," Heinrich said, running toward the portal. The other toys followed and jumped through.

Theo was last. He jumped toward the portal, but some of the lingering shadows had gathered. A hand snatched Theo's leg and pulled him into the ether.

Lucinda screamed, but it was too late.

Theo and Stratus tumbled into free fall, slashing at each other as the world crumbled around them. They fell for what seemed like an eternity until they landed on a shadowy floor. Darkness surrounded them.

Stratus rose, but he was breathing heavily. His body, previously pure shadow, was now fog and bone. Half his head was missing, and he only had one red eye now—the other was gone. He looked as if only a few blows would finish him forever.

"I'll never lose hope," Theo said. His sword glowed, and he ran at Stratus and slashed him relentlessly. He jumped into the air, and light gathered at the tip of his sword. He brought it down on Stratus's face, and the whole area flooded with light.

Stratus sputtered as bright light radiated from inside his body, and then exploded. Tatters of shadows floated down like feathers, and Theo knew that Stratus was no more.

The blackness melted around him and a portal appeared.

He jumped through and landed on the floor of the throne room. The toys cheered.

"We thought you were gone for sure," Lucinda said, helping him up.

"Never."

"Is he really gone now?"

Theo nodded.

There was a shimmer of light, and Grant appeared, sleeping on the floor. He opened his eyes and looked around sleepily.

"Theo?"

Theo rushed to his side and hugged him. "It's time to get out of here."

A gentler-looking portal appeared; Grant's bedroom was on the other side.

"Now is your chance," Lucinda said.

Theo faced the caravan. "Come back with me."

"We have to stay," Lucinda said. "We're going to rebuild the Stratusphere. There are thousands of toys here who are wondering what just happened. We can't leave them." She smiled. "Besides, all of us wouldn't fit in Grant's toy box."

"Lucinda—thanks."

The other toys gave him a group hug, and then held him up and cheered.

"One final cheer for Theo!"

"Oh god, yes!"

"Yesiree!"

They set him down, and Gasket licked him sadly. Theo patted him on the neck and said, "See you, pal."

He joined Grant at the portal. Grant jumped through, but when Theo jumped, the portal disappeared, and he crashed to the floor.

"No!" He punched the ground. "I can't believe it . . ."

Through a thin slit in the ceiling, they saw the first crack of sunlight.

Lucinda touched Theo's shoulder. "He's safe. You can be sure of that."

"How will I get home?"

"The link between our world and the human world is broken now. Stratus was the link, but now that he's dead, I don't know how to restore it."

Theo looked at Jiskyl. "Surely, you must know."

Jiskyl shook his head and turned away.

"Don't lose hope," Bethany said, dancing around him. "There has to be another portal in the castle somewhere."

Theo nodded and rushed toward the throne room door. "You're right. Let's go."

The ground shook, and the castle began to collapse around them.

Theo started down a hall, but Heinrich grabbed him. "We've got to get out of here, Theo."

"No—"

"You can search for a portal and die in the process, or you can save yourself and live," Heinrich said.

Theo stared down the hall, and the reality of being trapped hit him. He knew deep down that there weren't any more portals. He swallowed hard.

They ran as everything fell around them, barely escaping the castle. Once they were clear of its stone walls, they looked back as it caved in on itself, leaving a gigantic heap of rubble.

Meanwhile, the sun rose, painting the sky yellow and orange.

"I've been in the Stratusphere for a long time," Heinrich said, putting his hand over his heart, "And this is the first time I've seen the sun."

"Stratus really *is* dead," Bethany said. "I bet all the toys'll be shocked."

"They're probably scratching their heads," Jiskyl said.

Lucinda hovered in front of Theo and put on her best smile. "We'll find a way to get you home."

He didn't smile back; instead, he stared at the horizon, now a blaze of red and orange. "At least I protected Grant. I just hope he will be okay. I won't be there for him anymore."

"I'd say that if he can survive Stratus, the rest of life's perils will be nothing," Jiskyl said.

They walked toward a nearby town where toys were gathered in the streets.

Lucinda floated downhill toward the town. "To a new future!"

Theo looked at the clouds again and thought of Grant. He didn't feel the heaviness that had been in his heart since he came to the Stratusphere. It was hard to accept that he might never see Grant again, but at least Grant would be safe.

Heinrich hoisted him onto his shoulders and ran down the hill, shouting with joy. He reached up and tickled Theo's stomach, and for the first time in a long time, Theo let go of himself and laughed long and hard.

AFTERWORD

Festival of Shadows was inspired by an image I saw on Pinterest of a teddy bear fighting a huge monster while protecting his owner. It moved me. The image, beautifully drawn, said so much with no words at all. I couldn't get it out of my mind, and I knew that I had to write a story.

At first, this book was a thousand-word short story that languished on my computer for a very long time. I couldn't get it right. I decided on a whim to make it a Decision Select Novel, and it wrote itself—I wasn't prepared for how quickly and radically it evolved. It turned out to be a book that I knew I was meant to write. Funny how that happens.

A teddy bear is an unlikely protagonist, especially in today's fiction market where readers expect human heroes, and anything out of the ordinary doesn't sell. But I've always been fascinated by them because I grew up with one; I figured I might not be the only adult who still had a soft spot for an old friend.

My bear's name was Teddy. My grandmother purchased him from a catalog and gave him to me when I was born. He had brown fur, one round ear, one floppy ear, and a zipper down his back that I would hide stuff in when I didn't want my mom to find it. My first memory ever is lying in the crib with him at dawn, talking gibberish as he smiled back at me.

I still have Teddy today, though I haven't slept with him in many, many years. He has lost his nose and eyes, but his smile is still as bright as it was when I was a baby.

I keep him around because he was always there for me. An only child, I was bullied when I preferred to read instead of play sports. I was teased because I grew up in an interracial family, and I wasn't like the other black kids at school. You name it, I was probably teased for it.

My childhood was lonely—full of books and video games. But no matter how lonely I was, Teddy always listened to me when no one else would. He helped me cope with life as a kid. Like most kids who are attached to their favorite toys, I projected my fantasy emotions onto him. When I was shy, he was bold; when I was scared, he was strong; and when I despaired, he never lost hope. He was always braver and stronger than I could ever be. As I grew older, his tenacity rubbed off on me. Naturally, Teddy was the inspiration for Theo.

Inanimate objects make great characters. A writer can take the object, give it a spirit, and create a compelling conflict that is unique yet still familiar. Readers can see themselves in the character, and when the story is over, their hearts are bigger. If you never look at a toy the same way again after reading this book, then I've done my job.

I hope that you enjoyed Festival of Shadows as much as I enjoyed writing it. And if you're one of those peculiar people like me who still has a favorite toy, don't forget to thank it for its service.

READ NEXT: MAGIC SOULS

Here's an excerpt from *Magic Souls,* another one of Michael's novels. It's an interactive adventure for adults. If you loved Choose Your Own Adventures as a kid, you'll love this book.

MAGIC SOULS EXCERPT

CHAPTER 1
The Promotion Commotion

It was the morning of the biggest presentation of my legal career, and I spent ten minutes practicing my speech in front of a potted ficus. The bronze faces of the partners stared down at me from the wall, and I tried to imagine my face among them. If my presentation went well, I'd become a mid-level associate at the Hanover Law Firm—the most prestigious law firm in the city—and I'd finally get my own office instead of having to share a cubicle.

I hurried through the hall, swung into the conference room, and discovered that the meeting had begun without me. The partners sat around a long cedar table, watching a plasma TV mounted on the wall. They swiveled their heads toward me.

"You're late, Bebe," said Annette Farwell, my arch-nemesis with stilettos and perky breasts. Her designer suit made my blouse and skirt look like consignment items. She wasn't supposed to be in this meeting. She smirked at me from the head of the table, lacing her fingers together so that everyone could see her glittering maroon nails. "I've been working on this case for six months, and I don't appreciate you interrupting my presentation."

My PowerPoint slides hovered on the TV screen. Only at the Hanover Law Firm were the partners so busy that they couldn't tell when attorneys were stealing cases from each other.

I nearly turned green when I saw Tucker Salinas sitting at the table. He looked sexy in his black suit and red tie, and I could smell his lavender cologne across the room. His wavy hair and brown skin made him stick out in the room full of pasty white people like me.

"Wasn't this your case, Bebe?" he said.

"Well—"

Annette raised her voice to cover mine. "Of course Bebe helped me. When she wasn't on Facebook, she was wonderful. But time management is her weakness. It's just like her to be late."

I wanted to say, I'm late because you rescheduled the meeting without telling me, but what came out was something between a pout and a nervous laugh.

The managing partner shot up. "That's all I need. It's a tough decision—both of you do a great job. But on the basis of this case, Annette, we're going to go ahead and promote you to mid-level associate. Bebe, we'll discuss your performance at a later date."

Annette draped her palms over her mouth and sucked in air. "I can't thank you enough for recognizing my hard work." She schmoozed around the room, shaking everyone's hands. The partners ignored me as they filed out, and when I tried to meet Tucker's eyes, he looked through me, too.

"It's nothing personal," Annette said after the last attorney left. She primped her bun with one hand and packed her portfolio with the other. "You'll get your promotion in due time."

I blocked the door. "You stole my case."

"It's so nice to finally hear you speak. I couldn't tell if you were shocked, or if you were participating in one of your silent vegan protests again."

"This is wrong, Annette. You never worked on this case."

"You shouldn't have left your computer unlocked."

"You're committing fraud."

"You're the fraud." Annette stepped toward me. "And if you think I'm a bitch now," she said, "I dare you to tell the partners. Then I can tell them how you broke company protocol and kissed Tucker Salinas."

"How do you know that?"

Sure, I had kissed him. I'd had too many cocktails at happy hour—super embarrassing—but he hadn't kissed me back.

Annette saw me thinking and laughed. "You know the rules. Any kind of personal contact is grounds for termination. I'll make you wish that you'd dropped out of law school like you should have, and wonder why you didn't major in English, spend the rest of your life writing erotica, and contribute to society in some meaningful way other than being a tool for my personal advancement. Go on," she said, pointing to the door, "tell the partners."

I didn't know what to say. Annette pushed me aside and slammed the door behind her, leaving me alone with the lingering smell of cologne, legal pads, and betrayal.

* * *

The law firm was inside an old Victorian mansion. No one used the third floor because the partners hadn't brought the attic up to city code yet. It was dark and disorganized, with stacks of boxes and couches with plastic draped over them. A circular stained glass window gave the area an eerie light, as if it were haunted.

I liked to go there sometimes to think.

I sat on the landing and wiped my eyes. I kept thinking about how useless I was. Annette's words shouldn't have hurt me as much as they did, but I couldn't stop thinking about what she'd said. Maybe she was right. Maybe I had chosen the wrong profession.

"It's not fair," I said. "I wish I could go through life and be mean to people without facing consequences."

At that moment, a pile of boxes tumbled over, and glassware spilled out. I jumped up and scanned the darkness, but I didn't see anything. Maybe it was a rat. I got goosebumps, but at the same time it felt as if the temperature in the attic rose ten degrees.

I turned to go downstairs, but a tall, red-skinned demon in a suit and tie was standing in front of me. He had a long tail with a spade tip, and it circled behind him like an enchanted cobra. I nearly fainted when I saw him.

"I accept your offer," the demon said, grinning. His voice was deep and rich. "Annette is a real bitch, isn't she?"

I must have been hallucinating. "How'd you get in here?" I asked, blinking hard.

He straightened his tie and extended a hand. "Forgive me—I slide between dimensions so much that I often forget human formalities. My name is Ladouche."

"You're a demon, and I shouldn't be talking to you."

"But we just made a deal, Bebe. We've got to talk details."

"I never made a deal."

"A minute ago," the demon said, "didn't you say that you

wanted to 'go through life and be mean to people without facing consequences'?"

"Yes, but I wasn't serious—"

"Sure you were. Besides, I've already granted your wish." He gazed downstairs. "I'm tired of watching humans betray each other."

He put a finger on the banister and it burst into flames. The fire tore down to the first floor, where an attorney was standing with his elbow against the banister, talking on a cell phone. When the fire singed his elbow, the attorney leaped away and shouted every curse word there was, but for some reason, he never looked upstairs.

The banister returned to normal, and Ladouche laughed. "From now on, you can do whatever you want. Be mean, ruin someone's day. When you do, I guarantee that you won't get caught."

"W-why would I want to do that?"

He grinned again and closed his hands into fists. "Because you need your job; because you want revenge; because Annette will do this to you again if you let her."

"No."

"She isn't the first, Bebe. Shall we go through the list of the three hundred and seven people who have manipulated you throughout your twenty-six years of existence?"

"Seriously? That many people?" I didn't want to believe it; I didn't want to believe that any of this was happening.

Ladouche must have sensed my disbelief. "How about Jessica Ramirez, who threatened to spread false rumors about your nether parts if you didn't do her contract law homework?"

"She still failed, you know."

"Or Manny Singh," Ladouche continued, "who fooled you into trusting him, only to betray you during your legal internship? But for him, you would have obtained a full scholarship to law school. That was a seventy-thousand dollar mistake."

"How do you know that?"

"I know everything, and I also know this: the number of manipulations you will experience in your life will increase five-fold if you do not accept my offer."

"This is insane."

"I'll show you something insane," Ladouche said. He snapped his fingers, and a holographic screen hovered between us. Annette was on it; she was in the managing partner's office.

"If this is true," the managing partner said, "She has to go. We need Tucker."

"You know me," Annette said, "I wouldn't come to you if it weren't important—and true."

"No," I said. "She can't be—"

The screen disappeared, and Ladouche frowned. "In a few minutes, you'll be unemployed. How's that for insanity?"

I backed away and shook my head. "Fine. I don't have anything to hide. Yeah, I kissed him. That's not a crime, and if they fire me over some stupid firm policy, it's just as well. It's not worth the struggle."

Ladouche's eyes burst into circular flames. "You're pathetic. What will it take for you to stand up for yourself?"

"I don't know, but revenge isn't the answer." I was not going to give in to his temptation.

"Funny! Where'd you learn that? Church?"

I put my hands to my head and tried to shake him out of my vision, but he wouldn't go away.

"Go home, then," he roared. "Cry yourself to sleep, like you do every time someone exploits you. When you wake up tomorrow morning, you'll realize that Annette is twelve thousand dollars richer, and that your only chance for a promotion is gone. You'll have to go to another firm and start over. It'll take years, and along the way, others will use you, too. You'll look back on this moment and think, 'I should have listened to Uncle Ladouche. I should have gotten my revenge.' But by then, I'll be helping someone else and will have forgotten you entirely."

I backed down the stairs, too afraid to take my eyes off him, but he kept stepping toward me.

"If you don't stand up for yourself, Tucker will never notice you."

"That's none of your business," I said, trying not to show that his words stung. "You have no right to comment on my love life. Please leave, or I'll call the cops."

Ladouche bowed, scowling at me all the way down, and then he vanished, leaving a veil of golden smoke in the air. It choked me, and I had to run downstairs to escape it.

The managing partner was waiting outside his office as I came down the stairs.

"Bebe, we need to talk."

I couldn't deal with getting fired on top of everything else that had happened, so I pretended to keep coughing and ran past him, ducked into my cube for my purse, and kept running all the way out to the parking lot.

My mind was on autopilot as I drove home. The sun was setting behind the city skyline, and it lit the horizon with an orange and pink fire—the kind of fire I felt inside as I thought about Annette. I couldn't stop thinking about what had happened.

And Ladouche—as if the day couldn't get any stranger. Was he real? Could his promise really be true? I had to admit, it would be nice to push Annette out of the third floor window, and shrug my shoulders to the police when they asked me who did it . . .

I heard a horn and glanced up; an SUV was barreling toward me. I screamed as its headlights brightened the interior of my car. I froze as it loomed near, but at the last second, I jerked my wheel. I lost control as my car zigzagged across the intersection and jolted to a stop on the side of the road, facing oncoming traffic. I heard a BOOM, and saw the SUV on the other side of the road, against a guardrail. The driver, a woman with long hair, rubbed her forehead as smoke rose from the hood.

I looked back at the traffic signal and my heart stopped. My light had been red.

A squad car pulled up behind me.

Crap.

The officer was at my window in an instant. He wore a tan uniform emblazoned with the Hanover sheriff star. He tapped the window with his knuckle, and when I rolled it down, he hooked his fingers in his belt and rocked on his toes as he spoke. "You okay, Miss?"

"Officer, I'm so sorry—"

"For what?"

"I ran the red light." I handed my license to him, but he wouldn't accept it.

"No, the other car ran the red light. I saw it."

"But—"

"I just wanted to make sure you were okay."

He tipped his hat and left me dazed. The accident had been my fault; it was obvious. Why hadn't he given me a ticket?

I heard an "erh-hm" —Ladouche was in the passenger seat, reading a newspaper with a photo of the wrecked SUV on the front page, with a headline that said, UNINSURED

MOTORISTS ON THE RISE! PROMISING ATTORNEY NOT AT FAULT, GETS HUGE SETTLEMENT.

"Pretty impressive, yes?" he asked, folding the paper neatly into compartments.

I nearly jumped out of the car. "Seriously, stop appearing like that."

"Of course you ran the red light, Bebe, but no one will ever know."

"How could you?" I cried. "Look—that innocent woman is going to get a ticket because of your trick."

"Stop worrying about other people." He waved his hands and the windows frosted over, preventing me from seeing out. He shoved his face in front of mine and said, "Are you going to get your revenge or what?"

"You and revenge! What makes you think I want payback?"

"I'm giving you a once-in-a-lifetime opportunity, and you're going to ignore it? Hmph. Go ahead and add this moment to your list of greatest regrets. Farewell."

Ladouche began to dematerialize, but something deep inside me wanted him to stay. I was too upset to think clearly, and I gave in to my emotions.

"Wait," I said. "Do I really have immunity?"

He rematerialized and nodded.

"I'm not a vengeful person," I said. "I just . . . I just don't understand how she got away with it."

Ladouche leaned in. "It's not your job to understand."

I stared at the frosted glass and tried to ignore my conscience—it was surprisingly easy. "I accept."

He disappeared, but his laughter lingered as the windshield defrosted.

My mind kept settling back on Annette and her smug smile. Embarrassment welled up in the base of my stomach and gushed into my mouth; I wanted to hold it in, but I couldn't. I screamed long and loud, and when I stopped, I was shaking. I had never let my feelings out like this before, and it scared me.

What was I going to do? I had to make a decision.

Grab your copy of *Magic Souls* at www.michaellaronn.com/magicsouls.

ACKNOWLEDGMENTS

Cover Design: Kip Ayers

Copyeditor: Maya Packard

Proofreader: Calee Allen

Beta Readers: Rasana Atreya, Brian Darr, and Mark Phillips.

As always, I'd like to thank my wife for her support, and my family for their love.

MEET MICHAEL LA RONN

Science fiction and fantasy on the wild side!

Michael La Ronn is the author of many science fiction and fantasy novels including the Modern Necromancy, The Last Dragon Lord, and Sword Bear Chronicle series.

In 2012, a life-threatening illness made him realize that storytelling was his #1 passion. He's devoted his life to writing ever since, making up whatever story makes him fall out of his chair laughing the hardest. Every day.

Learn more about Michael
www.michaellaronn.com

MORE BOOKS BY MICHAEL LA RONN

Find more books by Michael La Ronn by visiting:

www.michaellaronn.com/books

Sign up for the Michael La Ronn Fan Club to receive updates about new releases, bonus content, and more at www.michaellaronn.com/fanclub.

Made in the USA
Columbia, SC
06 July 2024

38200685R00090